"You almo[...]
said starkly

Then suddenly Gabe had her in his arms, holding her in a desperate, almost painful grip, his face buried in her hair. Page clung to him, seeking something she was afraid to define.

His skin was so warm. She'd almost forgotten how the muscles rippled beneath the surface, how the coarseness of his hair contrasted so deliciously with the sleekness of his flesh.

His mouth closed over hers and Page lost herself in his kiss. Gabe worked his hands beneath her T-shirt to stroke her bare back. His palms were warm against her skin. Greedy. He wanted her. She had no doubt of that. But was there more? He had loved her once—did he still?

"Page," he said in a raspy voice. "I…"

She drew back to look at him, straining to see him in the darkness. She saw only the feverish glitter of his eyes. The hunger. The need.

A need that seemed to match her own.

Page ran a fingertip over his bottom lip. "I've missed you so much, Gabe. Will you make love to me…one last time?"

"Very seldom does a writer get a chance to revisit a favorite story line," says talented author **Gina Wilkins.** "But in writing *The Getaway Bride*, I got to do just that. In 1995 I wrote *I Won't* for Temptation's Grooms on the Run miniseries. The books were so popular that the editors decided to try it again—with a twist. I hope you enjoy *The Getaway Bride*, my contribution to Temptation's newest miniseries, Brides on the Run."

Books by Gina Wilkins

HARLEQUIN TEMPTATION
470—AS LUCK WOULD HAVE IT
486—JUST HER LUCK
501—GOLD AND GLITTER
521—UNDERCOVER BABY
539—I WON'T
567—ALL I WANT FOR CHRISTMAS
576—A VALENTINE WISH
592—A WISH FOR LOVE
620—A NIGHT TO REMEMBER

Don't miss any of our special offers. Write to us at the following address for information on our newest releases.

Harlequin Reader Service
U.S.: 3010 Walden Ave., P.O. Box 1325, Buffalo, NY 14269
Canadian: P.O. Box 609, Fort Erie, Ont. L2A 5X3

Gina Wilkins
THE GETAWAY BRIDE

Harlequin Books

TORONTO • NEW YORK • LONDON
AMSTERDAM • PARIS • SYDNEY • HAMBURG
STOCKHOLM • ATHENS • TOKYO • MILAN
MADRID • WARSAW • BUDAPEST • AUCKLAND

For John, my own hero and "technical adviser."
I couldn't do any of this without you.

ISBN 0-373-25733-3

THE GETAWAY BRIDE

Copyright © 1997 by Gina Wilkins.

_____Prologue_____

GABE CONROY SMILED as he headed up the walkway in the Austin, Texas, trailer park. He held a bouquet of flowers in his work-roughened left hand, on which he wore a new gold wedding ring. He'd stopped at the supermarket on his way home and chosen the blooms himself. The small bunch of carnations and daisies had cost him five ninety-five.

Someday, he told himself, he'd bring his wife roses. Just as, someday, he intended to give her a real honeymoon.

His wife. The words still startled him when they crossed his mind. He'd been a married man for exactly three weeks, after a whirlwind courtship of just nine weeks. They'd been the happiest three months of his entire life.

He stuck his key in the front door of the mobile home, sweeping his battered black Western hat off his sweat-dampened brown hair as he stepped inside. The familiar aroma of strawberries greeted him; his wife was a nut for strawberry-scented candles, he thought indulgently.

"Page? I'm home." His eager call seemed to echo in the trailer.

He hung his hat on the brass-plated stand by the door, next to the wide-brimmed straw hat Page often wore to protect her fair skin from the sun. Blond and blue-eyed, she burned easily, and was very careful to avoid overexposure.

Gabe was glad she wasn't one of those women who tanned her skin to resemble tough leather; he loved the velvety soft feel of her. Besides, too much sun was considered dangerous these days, and Gabe wouldn't want anything to harm his bride. He was taking his responsibilities as husband and protector very seriously, despite her teasing about his old-fashioned attitudes.

"Page?"

The tiny living room was impeccably neat. There was nothing out of place except the colorful paperback Page had been reading. The book was still lying on the sofa where she'd dropped it when he'd swept her into his arms and off to bed the night before. Gabe's grin deepened when he mentally replayed the interlude that had followed.

He headed for the bedroom. "Honey?"

The bed was made, and the door to the closet-size bathroom stood open, revealing polished fixtures but no Page. He wondered why she hadn't answered him. Even if she was in the kitchen, she'd have heard him.

She wasn't in the kitchen.

He set the flowers on the tabletop and rubbed the back of his neck, wondering where in the heck she'd gone. She'd have been home from work at least a couple of hours ago. Had she run to the grocery store for something?

When he'd parked his pickup at the curb, he hadn't thought to look in the metal carport behind the trailer to see if Page's little Dodge was there. He looked through the kitchen window. Sure enough, the carport was empty.

He frowned. Though he certainly didn't expect her to report her every movement, she usually let him know when she'd be out, so he wouldn't worry. He'd already gotten into the habit of doing the same, calling when he would be late or checking with her before making plans. They'd agreed that such mutual courtesy would be part of their marriage routine.

A covered basket on the counter caught his eye. He lifted the cloth napkin and sniffed appreciatively. Mrs. Dooley's homemade bread, still slightly warm from the oven. He'd bet Mrs. Dooley would know where Page had gone.

He stepped outside and crossed the tiny lot to the one next door. He knocked briskly on the back door of a blue and white trailer almost identical to his own.

A heavyset woman with frizzy gray hair and smiling brown eyes opened the door. "Well, hello, Gabe. Page send you to borrow a cup of sugar?"

"Actually, I wanted to ask if you've seen Page. I just got home and she isn't there."

Mrs. Dooley chuckled. "You newlyweds. Can't stand to let each other out of sight for a few minutes."

Gabe smiled sheepishly. "I suppose I've gotten

spoiled. I'm used to having her greet me when I get home from work."

His neighbor patted his arm. "Don't you go smotherin' the girl, now. She needs a little breathing space."

"I know. Guess I overreacted. But she should have been home hours ago. When I saw your bread on the counter, I thought she might have told you where she was going. By the way, thanks. You know how I love your bread."

"Why do you think I made an extra loaf? Makes me feel good to know how much you enjoy it. I carried it over about an hour ago, and Page was there then. We didn't get a chance to talk much. She had just thanked me for the bread when the telephone rang. It looked like she was having a serious conversation, so I signaled that I'd talk to her later and came on home."

Gabe wondered who had called, but he figured Page'd tell him later if she wanted him to know. "Thanks again for the bread, Mrs. Dooley," he said as he moved away.

"You're welcome, hon. And don't you be eatin' it all up before Page gets home, you hear? I made it for both of you."

He grinned. "Then she'd better hurry home."

Mrs. Dooley laughed and shook her head as she closed her door.

THE BREAD was still sitting untouched on the counter two hours later. Gabe paced the trailer, torn between worry and anger. Damn it, where was Page? It wasn't like her to go off like this.

He thought of Mrs. Dooley's advice to give Page breathing room. But it wasn't as if he would have forbidden her to leave if she'd told him she had plans.

He expected her to have friends. Outside interests. Just because they hadn't spent more than a few hours at a time apart since they'd met three months ago didn't mean he planned to keep her shackled to the trailer. But surely Page knew he would worry if she just disappeared like this, with no explanation, no forewarning, nothing.

He picked up the phone and dialed Page's best friend, Betty Anne Spearman. Betty Anne and Page were both teachers at a local elementary school. Betty Anne could tell him if something had come up at school, though Gabe found it hard to believe his wife wouldn't have called him if there had been a change of plans.

Betty Anne hadn't heard from Page. Nor had Page told her about any plans she'd had for the evening. Betty Anne agreed that it wasn't like Page to be inconsiderate or absentminded. "I'm worried, Gabe," she said. "Are you sure she didn't tell you where she'd be this evening?"

"I'm sure," he answered grimly. "In fact, we'd planned to go out to a movie tonight. We talked about it at breakfast this morning. She seemed to be looking forward to it."

"Oh, Gabe, this doesn't sound good. Do you...do you think you should call the police?"

His stomach tightened. "Let's not panic," he said, trying to calm himself as much as her. "She'll probably be home soon."

"You'll have her call me when she gets in? Just to set my mind at rest?"

"Yeah, Betty Anne, I'll have her call."

He hung up the phone and started pacing again. Tiny kitchen. Minuscule living room. Narrow hallway. Small bedroom.

It was hardly a palace he'd brought his bride home to, he thought wryly, but she hadn't seemed to mind. She'd assured him she would be very happy here, at least until they could afford a bigger place for themselves and the children they both wanted.

Cash was tight now, but Page seemed convinced it was only a matter of time until his fledgling business was a success. The faith she had in him was one of the things he loved most about her.

Gabe had already asked an architect buddy to start drawing up some plans for a three-bedroom house that he wanted to build as soon as he was sure his construction company was securely established—which, he hoped, wouldn't be much longer. Business had been good lately. *Life* had been good, as far as Gabe was concerned.

Now, if only he could find his wife....

He tried to think of someone else to call. Page had no family, and not many friends in this area. Her parents had been dead for several years and Gabe remembered being surprised that she'd been on her own a long time, though she was only twenty-five. He admired her self-sufficiency, even if he found her deeply ingrained independence a bit daunting at times.

Without much optimism, he called his mother and his sister, Annie. Neither had heard from Page. Both expressed concern that she'd been missing now for more than three hours.

He called the pastor of the church that Page attended faithfully. Reverend Morgan had married Page and Gabe in a tiny private ceremony in the church sanctuary, with little fanfare and only a handful of witnesses.

Page had called it the most beautiful wedding any woman could have wanted.

"I haven't heard from her, Gabe," the minister stated gravely. "Page isn't a thoughtless person. Have you considered contacting the authorities?"

Gabe thanked the man for his concern, his advice, and his promise of prayer. And then he hung up the phone and buried his face in his hands.

He wasn't sure what made him suddenly stand and walk back into the bedroom. He rounded the bed, which took up most of the meager floor space, and stumbled over something at the foot. Looking down, he spotted Page's slippers. He picked one up, cradling the little satin shoe in his big, calloused hand. And then he opened the closet door.

It was immediately apparent that some of Page's clothes were missing. Not all of them; it looked as though she'd grabbed a few at random and stuffed them into the overnight bag that usually rested on the top shelf. The bag wasn't there now.

He could feel his heart start to pound, slowly, painfully. There was a strange buzzing in his ears, like the sound of an annoying insect. Or a nagging premonition.

Stiff with dread, he opened the top drawer of the built-in bureau, the one in which Page kept her lingerie. It was empty, except for the small white envelope with his name scrawled across the front. It was all he could do to pick it up.

She hadn't wanted him to find it too quickly, he realized dully. Why?

The note was brief, the writing hastily scrawled.

Gabe,
I'm so sorry. I can't explain now, but I have to leave you. I know this will be hard for you to understand, but I'm doing this for your sake. Don't try to find me. I can't be with you now. Please believe that I never meant to hurt you. I'm so very sorry.

Page.

Gabe sank slowly to the edge of the bed, staring at the nearly incomprehensible note that seemed to become more blurry the longer he looked at it. It was a very long time before he moved again.

I have to leave you. The words had sliced deeply into

him. As he sat there, trying to understand them, the remnants of his youth bled from the wound. Not quite thirty, he had just lost the fire and enthusiasm with which he'd once faced the future.

His bride had taken away much more than her clothing when she left him.

1

PAULA SMITHERS wasn't exactly popular with the people she saw on a daily basis, and she knew it. In fact, she encouraged it. She went out of her way to hold them at more than arm's length.

She had no place in her life for friends.

Every morning at exactly 8:00 a.m., she reported to work in the back office of a car dealership in Des Moines, Iowa, where she efficiently processed paperwork in almost undisturbed solitude for eight hours a day, five days a week. The sales staff contacted her only to give instructions and ask questions, and the other employees had given up trying to make her part of their friendly group after their early efforts had been firmly rebuffed.

Paula was never actually rude to the others, but she made no effort to be particularly friendly, either. After five months here, she was convinced that her coworkers considered her an eccentric loner with no social life and little personality. She had worked hard to create that facade.

Occasionally, some well-intentioned individual would try to reach her. Invite her to lunch. Make an effort to befriend her out of pity or kindness. Paula had her response down pat. A cool smile and an unwaveringly brusque rejection of any friendly overture.

The barriers she placed between herself and the others were invisible, but obvious nonetheless. Eventually, even the warmest-hearted do-gooder conceded defeat and left her to her requested isolation.

Blake Jones, the newest sales associate at the dealership, was proving to be more tenacious than the others had been.

"'Morning, Paula," he said, sauntering into her cubbyhole office with a stack of paperwork. "Don't you look nice today."

She was wearing a brown jacket dress that made her skin look sallow and did nothing to enhance her brown eyes. She hadn't tried to soften the severity of the look with jewelry; she wore only a plain, leather-banded watch on her left wrist and a thin gold chain that disappeared beneath the high collar of her unflattering dress.

She'd pulled her mousy hair into a severe bun that would have been more suited to a woman twice her age. She wore no makeup, and her oversize glasses had slid down her short nose again, forcing her to push at them with her forefinger. Well aware of every detail of her carefully constructed appearance, Paula put little credence into Blake's compliment.

"Thank you," she said coolly, reaching for the forms. Her tone implied that the conversation ended there.

Blake didn't take the hint. He'd worked for McElden Motors for just two weeks and had already broken all existing records for the most car sales made in the first month of employment. Tenacity was a plus in sales, of course, but he seemed to carry the trait over into everything else he did. And for some reason, he'd been determined to befriend Paula, despite her resistance.

She'd sensed from the beginning that his interest in her was not sexual. A woman usually suspected when a man was genuinely attracted to her, and Paula knew that wasn't the case with Blake. Yet he continued to try his best to draw her out. She could only guess his motive to be pity—or conceit. Perhaps he was the type of man who simply couldn't stand it if a woman didn't succumb to his considerable charms.

He was definitely attractive. Boyishly tousled golden hair. Wicked blue eyes. Killer smile. A slender physique that nicely set off his penchant for loose shirts and softly pleated slacks. A thirty-something heart-throb.

He had no way of knowing, of course, that Paula's heart had long been locked away in a place where no one would ever make it throb again.

"I was thinking about trying out that new Chinese place down the street for lunch today," he said. "Would you like to join me?"

"No, thank you," she murmured, deliberately turning her attention back to her work. "I brought my lunch."

Resting one lean hip against the edge of her desk, he picked up her stapler, tape dispenser and a brass paperweight and absently began to juggle them. Paula's eyebrows lifted as she watched the heavy items arc lazily through the air.

"It's a beautiful day," he said enticingly. "It's finally starting to look like spring. Much too nice for a brown-bag sandwich. Wouldn't you rather get out of the office for an hour or so?"

"No. I'd rather eat in," she said firmly.

She was momentarily diverted when he skillfully shifted into a new pattern of tossing the desk accessories from one hand to the other. "You missed your calling," she couldn't resist saying. "You should have joined the circus."

He stilled his hands and replaced her possessions on the desk. The sleeve of his pale blue shirt pulled back when he reached out, revealing a glimpse of what might have been a small tattoo on his right wrist. Before Paula could identify it, he'd hidden it again beneath his cuff.

"Been there. Done that," he said without elaboration. "Last chance for Chinese?"

She shook her head. He heaved an exaggerated sigh and sauntered toward the doorway. She'd noticed that Blake rarely seemed to move in a hurry.

"Some other time, then," he said.

She didn't respond. She had no intention of having lunch with him at any time, but she didn't want to issue a challenge by saying so now. He would lose interest in her soon, she assured herself. They all did, after a while.

Ignoring the hollow ache of loneliness inside her, she

turned her thoughts firmly back to her paperwork. She was very good at her job.

It was all she had.

PAULA STOPPED at a take-out Chinese restaurant on her way home that evening, ordering egg drop soup and cashew chicken. She'd been craving Chinese food ever since Blake had asked her out for lunch.

Carefully balancing her dinner, she unlocked the front door of her tiny furnished apartment that was tucked into one secluded corner of an uninspired, moderately priced complex. The apartment was quiet and empty, as always. The furnishings were bland and inexpensive and she hadn't bothered with accessories or bric-a-brac.

She never had visitors, so it didn't matter if the place was dull and gloomy. More cheerful and tasteful decor wouldn't have made a difference to Paula; the bleakness she carried inside her would have prevented her from fully appreciating even the most elegant surroundings.

She set her dinner on the tiny round table in her kitchenette, pushing a newspaper and the day's mail to one side. The glasses she didn't need lay on top of the mail. She'd been relieved, as always, to find only advertising fliers and an electric bill in her mailbox.

Except for bills and junk mail, her box was usually empty. She received no magazines, no personal letters. Yet checking her mail was undoubtedly the most stressful activity in her rigid daily routine.

She ate her dinner, cleared away the remains and then went into her bedroom to change out of the dress she'd worn to work and into a soft sleep shirt. She pulled the pins out of her hair, and the severe bun fell apart. Her thick hair tumbled to her shoulders as though relieved to be released from confinement. She combed her fingers through it, looking in the mirror for signs that the drab color needed retouching.

She washed her face, brushed her teeth, and took out her brown-tinted contact lenses, storing them carefully in their case. She glanced into the mirror over the sink and grimaced at her blue-eyed reflection. She often had the unsettling feeling that the ghost of a past life was looking back at her from behind the glass.

She spent the remainder of the evening ensconced on her sofa with a paperback novel and a bowl of strawberry ice cream. The television was on, but she paid no attention to the program. She'd turned it on only for the comforting sound of human voices.

It was the only companionship she had allowed herself for more than two years.

IT INFURIATED GABE that his hand wasn't quite steady when he reached across his desk to accept the photographs Blake offered him. He would have liked to believe that Blake didn't notice, but he suspected that very few details escaped the man's deceptively lazy-looking gaze.

Gabe studied the photographs closely. They were candid snapshots, taken without the subject's knowledge. The woman pictured was hardly spectacular. She appeared to be in her early to mid-thirties. She looked stern and humorless. Mousy hair. Brown eyes. Heavy glasses. Unflattering clothing.

Page would be almost twenty-eight now. Her hair had been a rich honey-blond, her eyes the pure blue of a clear summer sky. She'd had a weakness for pretty clothes in bright colors. Her smiles had been sweet, a bit shy, and while there'd occasionally been shadows in her beautiful eyes, she'd never looked as unrelentingly grim as the woman in these photographs.

It had been two and a half years since she'd walked out on him.

"Well?" Blake prodded from across the desk, a hint of sympathy in his voice.

Gabe sighed and nodded, his gaze riveted to the pale face in the photograph he was holding in his left hand. The hand on which he still wore the ring Page had put there on their wedding day.

"Yes," he said heavily. "This is my wife."

He lifted his head to look fiercely at the blond man. "Where is she?"

PAULA WAS ALWAYS tense when she looked through her mail, never knowing what she would find, but this Saturday morning seemed worse than usual for some reason. She tried to reassure herself that there was no reason for more than the usual concern. But there was one small detail that worried her.

Blake Jones had disappeared.

Without even calling his employer, he'd simply not shown up for work two days ago—the day after Paula had declined his invitation for lunch. No one had heard a word from him since.

Being someone who knew all about disappearing without notice—and the many reasons a person could be driven to do so—Blake's vanishing act bothered Paula. Mostly, she worried that it had something to do with her.

She didn't waste time calling herself paranoid. She, more than most, had every reason to be anxious.

The fact was that Blake had seemed unusually interested in her. And, since she'd determined he wasn't after her body, she couldn't help but worry about what he *had* been after.

Distracted by her nervous speculation, she flipped through the junk mail without interest, tossing the colorful flyers away without bothering to read them. She set the water bill and cable bill aside to pay later. Since television and books were the only entertainment she allowed herself, she ordered as many channels as she could afford.

The final envelope made the blood drain from her face.

It was addressed to Paula Smithers, complete with apartment number and correct zip code. There was no return address, but the oddly slanted handwriting was sickeningly recognizable to her.

She knew exactly what she would find inside. Photographs. Nothing else. No note of explanation or identification.

Her hands were shaking so hard she could hardly open the flap. Two snapshots tumbled out when she finally ripped the envelope apart.

The photos blurred in front of her eyes as she reached out to touch a fingertip to a face she hadn't seen in two and a half years. And then she recognized the subject of the other photograph. Her breath caught in a painful sob.

"Oh, God," she whispered, groping for the back of the nearest chair for support. "Oh, God."

It took several long moments to fight off the dizziness and the nausea. And then she leaped into action, snatching up the photographs and hurrying into her bedroom.

She pulled out the large suitcase that was always kept in readiness, and began to fill it haphazardly, going through motions that had become all too common in the past thirty-odd months. She didn't bother with the few plain suits and other work clothing, but grabbed jeans, tops, sweatsuits, socks and underwear. Practical, sturdy, easy-care clothing that required little attention, and could be donned swiftly.

Paula Smithers, aka Page Shelby Conroy, was on the run again.

GABE ALMOST MISSED her.

He'd been sitting in his pickup for at least fifteen minutes in the parking lot of the apartment complex

Blake had directed him to. He'd been trying to get up his nerve to knock on her door, mentally rehearsing the questions he would ask her, the scathing words he wanted to say to her.

Taking advantage of the nice weather on this April weekend morning, two buff, young guys were meticulously washing and waxing a classic '67 Mustang in a corner of the lot. Gabe was aware that they had noticed him sitting there. They probably wondered why he hadn't gotten out of his truck.

He drew a deep breath, opened his door and climbed out. He had just taken a step toward the building when he spotted a woman hurrying down the walk, dragging a wheeled suitcase behind her.

Had he not seen the photographs, he might not have recognized her. She looked very different from the woman who had haunted his dreams for so long. He was well aware that he had changed, too, though his own changes were mostly internal.

He frowned at the sight of her suitcase. It was obvious that she was running again. But why? Had she somehow been tipped off that he'd located her? And if so, why the hell was she so determined to avoid him?

What in God's name had he done to her?

He stepped in front of her, blocking her way. "Hello, Page."

Her face had already been ashen. At the sight of him, it bleached to a deathly pallor. He grimly identified her expression as horror-stricken.

Her mouth opened, but nothing came out. She seemed literally unable to speak.

His automatic response to her obvious distress was concern. The protective instincts he'd almost forgotten kicked in, and he was about to say something to reassure her. Then he remembered the hell she'd put him through, and a wave of hurt and fury crashed though him.

"Don't look at me like that, damn it," he snapped. "I have a right to some answers."

"Please," she managed to say, her voice thin, breathless. "You have to leave. You have to go *now*."

He scowled. "I'll leave when I'm ready. First, you're going to answer my questions."

She shook her head, edging to one side of the walkway as though prepared to bolt around him. He saw her gaze shift quickly from him to the parking lot, obviously gauging the distance to her car.

"Please, Gabe," she whispered. "Go home."

"Home?" he repeated bitterly, thinking of that torturous afternoon two and a half years ago when he'd returned home so eagerly only to have his dreams smashed. "You really think I'm going to leave that easily now that I've found you?"

"You have to," she insisted, an edge of hysteria in her voice. "Leave me alone. I don't want you near me."

He was rather surprised to discover that she could still hurt him. He'd thought she'd done all the damage she could do the day she'd walked out on him. It seemed he'd been wrong.

"*Why,* Page?" he demanded roughly. "What did I do to you?"

She shook her head. "I have to go."

She moved to step around him.

Gabe reached out instinctively to stop her, his hand closing around her upper arm, which felt thinner than he remembered. His touch wasn't gentle, but he didn't harm her. Even as hurt and angry as he was, he would never use his size against her.

And yet, the moment he touched her, Page began to scream.

"What the—" Gabe began.

"Hey!" The two young men who'd been pampering the Mustang dropped their chamois cloths and sprinted toward them.

"Let go of her, mister!" one of them shouted.

Gabe automatically released his grip, and held his hands nonthreateningly away from her. "I'm not hurting her," he said. "She's—"

Page was already running, the suitcase bumping along behind her.

"Please," she gasped to her would-be rescuers as she passed them. "Hold him here for a few minutes. Just long enough for me to get away."

Gabe's instinctive movement after her was cut off when one of the guys took him down in a graceful tackle that must have been perfected through years of football training. Gabe's breath left him in a hard whoosh when he hit the concrete, the muscular young man on top of him.

He struggled to get up. "Let go of me, damn it. She's my *wife!*" he said furiously.

Desperation added strength to his movements. If he lost her now, who knew how long it would be until he located her again? If ever.

"Dave, help me!" the guy on top of him yelled. "I can't hold him by myself."

The other young man promptly threw himself on top of the mini pile. The commotion had drawn attention from other apartments. Already others were rushing to help—or to gawk.

"Give me at least fifteen minutes," Page called from her car. A car Gabe recognized—he'd helped her pick it out the week before the wedding.

"Page, stop!" Gabe shouted after her, momentarily ignoring the others. "Don't do this. I only want to talk to you—"

The roar of her car engine drowned out his words.

2

PAGE HAD NO DESTINATION in mind when she left Des Moines. She drove aimlessly, almost blindly, south. When she passed the car dealership where she'd worked for the past five months, she didn't even glance back.

She'd driven away from so many different places in the past thirty months that it barely caused her a pang to do so now. She would call Monday and let someone know she wouldn't be back. Her employer would be angry, but no one would worry about her enough to list her as a missing person. They would simply assume that she'd rudely quit without notice.

She doubted that anyone ever missed her when she made these abrupt moves. They missed her efficiency, perhaps, but not her. She'd made sure of that. There was only one person in the past two and a half years who'd probably grieved for her when she'd left, and she'd told herself that he'd gotten over her long ago.

Out of habit, she touched the thin gold chain at her throat, where it disappeared beneath the collar of her shirt. She still couldn't believe that Gabe had found her. She'd nearly had a heart attack when he'd stepped in front of her on that walkway. It had been like seeing a ghost.

Or like seeing a long-mourned part of herself.

How had he found her? How long had he been searching for her? And what was the connection between running into him and the photographs that had arrived in her mail? Both incidents had occurred the same day. Was it simply a bizarre twist of fate—or was it something much more sinister?

She tried to calm herself by focusing on the music coming from the cassette deck. And then she realized what song was playing. Sawyer Brown's Mark Miller was warning her that even the quickest way wasn't fast enough when you run from love.

She turned off the stereo and reached up to wipe at her face, finding it wet. She didn't know how long she'd been driving with tears streaming down her face. She swallowed a sob. She wouldn't cry. She never allowed herself to cry.

She forced herself to concentrate on her driving. Though she had little regard for her own life these days, as cold and empty as it had become, she was desperately determined not to cause harm to anyone else. That sole motivation had kept her alone and on the run for more than two years.

KEEPING IN TOUCH by cellular phone, Blake and Gabe caught up with Page in Wichita, Kansas, several hours after she'd escaped Gabe in Des Moines.

Gabe couldn't help but be impressed with Blake; the

guy seemed to have an almost psychic ability to locate Page. The other two detectives Gabe had previously hired had not been nearly as efficient.

As though sensing that he'd be needed, Blake had been nearby when Gabe had gone to confront Page at her apartment. He'd seen what had happened with the young men who'd rushed to "rescue" her from Gabe, and had followed Page at a discreet distance when she'd left town.

When she'd checked into a motel in Wichita, Blake had taken a room directly across from hers where he could keep an eye on things until Gabe arrived.

Her only stop, Blake informed his client after Gabe had slipped discreetly into his room, had been at a small pharmacy just inside the Wichita city limits. She'd emerged with a small plastic bag and had driven straight to this motel. She hadn't been out of her room since.

Gabe paced the cramped motel room like an enraged panther, his blood pounding in his ears.

"Why did she look at me that way when I tried to talk to her?" he demanded. "Why did she scream and run when I touched her arm?"

Sprawled in a chair by the window, his fingers templed in front of him, Blake watched Gabe's movements with searching eyes. "You said she acted terrified to see you. What threat do you pose to her?"

"None," Gabe insisted, throwing up his hands for emphasis. "I never laid a hand on her. Never even raised my voice to her. Hell, we weren't married long enough to have our first fight. There's no reason on earth for her to fear me."

He'd said similar words to the Des Moines police when they'd arrived at the summons of the apartment dwellers who'd acted as though he were an ax murderer. He'd told them that Page was his wife, that he'd only wanted to talk to her, that she hadn't given him a chance to speak—much less frighten her—before she'd started screaming for help.

The police had been suspicious, but there'd been no reason to hold him, particularly since Page had disappeared. His record had checked out clean, of course, and there was no one to file a formal complaint against him. He'd been released with a stern warning not to cause any further trouble.

Blake continued to watch him. "There must be something," he mused. "Did she take any money when she left you? Any valuable personal belongings? Is she worried that you want to charge her with theft? Did you tell me everything when you hired me?"

"She didn't take anything from me," Gabe answered wearily. *Nothing tangible, anyway*, he added to himself. "She didn't even pack all her own things. As for money, there wasn't any to steal. Nearly everything I had at that time was invested in the business."

Just as nearly everything he'd made since then had been spent locating Page.

"Then why is she so afraid of you finding her?"

"*I don't know!*" Frustrated, Gabe slammed the side of

his fist against the nearest wall, making the framed print hanging there rattle against the plaster.

He took a deep breath, trying to regain his precarious control over his temper. "I would have asked her, but she didn't hang around long enough," he said.

Blake rubbed his chin. "I'll tell you, Gabe, I've never seen a case quite like this one. There's always some reason for people to deliberately disappear. A crime they've committed, a secret they're hiding, fear of danger, something."

He shook his head. "I can't find anything in your wife's past to account for the way she's been living—alone, with no luxuries, no visible pleasures. It doesn't make sense."

"She once told me she'd led a very normal, uneventful life," Gabe said.

During the past months, he'd replayed nearly every conversation he and Page had had during their time together, searching for any clue as to where she might have gone, or why. He'd remembered nothing out of the ordinary.

Blake nodded. "That's what my research indicated. Born in Alabama, only child of a couple who married in their late thirties. Her father died in a car accident when she was in high school, and her mother passed away from cancer the summer after Page graduated. Page attended a university in Alabama on a full academic scholarship. She was a good student. No reports of her being in any trouble. The only discordant note on her record was a sexual harassment complaint she filed against a professor during her senior year."

So far, Blake wasn't giving Gabe any information he didn't already know. "She told me about that."

"Apparently, it was an ugly incident. The guy was eccentric, but popular with his students, and had seemed happily married for years. But whatever evidence Page presented to the administration must have been enough to get him fired. I wondered if maybe that incident had something to do with her actions now, but the professor died four years ago."

Gabe shook his head. "Page didn't like to talk about it. She said it was an ordeal that was very painful for her. But she seemed to consider it well behind her. She wasn't afraid when she told me about it, only sorry that it had happened."

Page had accepted another scholarship in Houston after her graduation from the Alabama university, he knew. There, she'd worked and studied for two more years, earning her master's degree in education. She'd sent résumés to several school districts afterward, and had found employment in Austin, specializing in teaching English as a second language.

An Austin native, Gabe had been introduced to Page through a mutual friend almost two years after she'd moved to the area. Nine weeks later, he'd married her. Three weeks after that, she'd vanished, leaving only a bewildering note of regret behind.

Twelve weeks, he thought dismally. The full extent

of his time with Page. And yet his life had changed irrevocably in those few traumatic weeks.

"The sexual harassment complaint probably has nothing to do with her movements now," Blake conceded, breaking into Gabe's grim musings. "It happened long before she met you. The professor was already dead by the time you and Page married. He shot himself, I understand."

Gabe digested that unsettling news with mixed emotions. Page hadn't told him that part. Had she known about the professor's fate?

"Something made her run out on me the way she did," he murmured. "It must be something drastic to account for the strange way she's been living since. But what?"

Blake shrugged, looking almost as frustrated as Gabe felt. "Short of mental illness, I can't come up with any theory as to why she's behaving this way."

"Mental illness?" Gabe stared at the other man. "You don't think Page is...unbalanced?"

"You have to admit her actions aren't exactly normal."

Gabe shook his head. "No," he said, remembering the Page he'd known and loved. Thinking of the woman he'd seen all too briefly that very afternoon.

She'd looked frightened, but she'd known exactly what she was doing when she screamed for help, detaining him long enough for her to get away. He couldn't understand why she was evading him, but he didn't for a minute believe she was demented. He simply couldn't accept it.

"No," he said again flatly. "She has a reason for what she's doing. And I intend to find out what it is."

"I think you're right," Blake admitted. "I worked with her for two weeks, and I would be willing to bet that she's as sane as you or I. But it doesn't take a genius to figure out that something is very wrong in her life."

Gabe only nodded. Something was very wrong in his life, too, he mused.

He was a married man without a wife.

Blake drew a deep breath, as though bracing himself for Gabe's reactions to his next words. "Gabe, I followed her here because I figured you'd want me to. But are you really sure it was the right thing to do?"

Gabe spun around to frown at the P.I. "What do you mean, the right thing? That's why I hired you. I heard you were the best."

Blake didn't bother to comment on his reputation. It seemed he accepted it as fact, rather than flattery. "It's obvious that she doesn't want to see you or talk to you. Maybe—"

"She's my *wife*."

"She left you two and a half years ago. For all she knows, you've dissolved the marriage."

"I haven't. And there's no record of her doing so, either. Sure, I've thought of just putting an end to it, forgetting about her, and getting on with my life. My friends and family have certainly tried to convince me to do so for the past couple of years. But I can't, Blake. Not without getting some answers. Not without knowing what went wrong. I just can't."

Blake sat in silence for several long moments, seeming to digest Gabe's words. "I wouldn't be able to, either," he confessed finally. "Like you, I'd have to know. So, you'll try again to ask your questions."

"And this time, damn it, she's going to answer them," Gabe said flatly.

Blake didn't look as certain. "And if she starts to scream again?"

"I'll deal with it." *Somehow.*

Blake glanced out the window, at the closed door across the way. "Good luck."

"Thanks. I'm going to need it."

SETTING HER HAIR DRYER on the counter, Page looked in the mirror of the motel bathroom. A pair of scissors sat at one side of the sink; she'd used them to crop her shoulder-length hair into a shorter cut that now fluffed around her face. Her former mousy-brown hair was a rich auburn now, shot with red.

It paid to invest in good hair colorings, she thought with weary satisfaction. As many times as she'd dyed her hair in the past months, she'd learned which brands worked best.

She left her brown contact lenses in. Her eyes looked darker with her hair this color. Paula Smithers had worn little or no makeup, so Page now emphasized her eyes with shadow, liner and mascara, and stroked blusher on her cheeks.

With a dark lipstick, she thought, studying the mirror, no one would recognize her as the mousy bookkeeper from Des Moines.

She didn't ask herself if the changes were necessary; it had become habit to alter her appearance as often as she changed addresses. If only it were as easy to shed the memories and emotions that followed to haunt her wherever she lived, whatever name she used.

She drew a deep breath and turned away from the mirror. She would spend the night here, then move on tomorrow, she decided. She hadn't decided where she would go. She would just get in her car and drive.

Maybe she'd go south again. Georgia or Mississippi or Louisiana.

Not that it mattered. Wherever she went, eventually the photographs would appear in the mail and she would have to move on.

And now she had to worry about Gabe finding her, too. He'd found her once. Could he do so again?

After what she'd done to him this time, would he bother to try?

She remembered the look in his eyes when he'd confronted her. Oh, yes. He would try.

Gabe Conroy was a determined man. Everything he'd ever wanted, he'd gone after with single-minded determination. His college education. His business. Her.

She shivered and pulled the lapels of her robe together as a cold wave of fear washed through her. Somehow, she had to convince Gabe to stay away from her.

She sighed and glanced at the uncomfortable-looking bed. It was still early, just after eight o'clock. She hadn't had dinner, but she wasn't very hungry. She should try to get some rest. She wanted to get an early start in the morning. Yet she dreaded going to sleep.

Her dreams were not pleasant ones these days.

A quiet rap on her door made her gasp and cover her mouth with her hands. Who—

"Page. Open the door."

She knew his voice, of course. Like a rapier, it sliced straight into her heart.

"Page?" He knocked again. "I know you're in there. Open up."

She stood frozen in the center of the small room, staring at the door, trying desperately to think of what to do. Would he go away if she refused to answer?

"Open this door or I swear I'll break it down."

He didn't raise his voice, but she heard him clearly enough. He wasn't bluffing. Even through the wood, she recognized the resolve in his tone.

Whatever the consequences, he was fully prepared to break the door in.

She took a deep breath and opened the door, leaving the safety chain in place. "Go away or I'll call the police."

Frowning at her through the narrow opening, he

glanced at her new hairstyle, then at her face. "Fine. Call them," he said.

He seemed to know her threat was an empty one. Maybe he suspected that she was as reluctant to call the police as he was for her to do so.

She tried another tactic. "I don't know who you think I am, but you're mistaken. I've never seen you before."

"I know exactly who you are," Gabe returned, his expression grim. "You're my wife."

Her breath caught in the back of her throat. She shook her head. "You're wrong. I'm nobody's wife."

"Let me in, Page."

"I'm *not* Page. Now go away."

He caught the door with his left hand when she would have closed it. The wedding ring she'd placed on his finger gleamed, catching her eye, holding her almost mesmerized. She hadn't expected that he would still be wearing it.

"I won't leave until we've talked," he said flatly. "Either let me in or there's going to be an ugly scene."

She heard footsteps approaching on the concrete walkway. She could call for help again, she thought rapidly. Would it work twice? Or would she be caught up with him by police interference, detained for precious hours, taking the risk of having public attention brought to her?

Gabe glanced in the direction of the footsteps, then back at her. "What's it going to be?" he asked quietly.

She swallowed hard and released the safety chain, praying that she was making the right choice.

She backed quickly away from the door, her arms locked defensively in front of her. She felt uncomfortably vulnerable in her robe and bare feet. She wished she'd had the chance to dress before dealing with this.

Gabe stepped into the room and closed the door behind him.

And then he just stood there, looking at her.

Her fingers tightened around the sash of her robe. Her throat was so tight that she couldn't have spoken even had she known what to say.

He looked older, she thought. He'd aged more than he should have in two and a half years.

His rich brown hair was still thick, still untouched by gray. He looked strong and fit, the picture of health and virility. A thirty-two-year-old man at his peak. And yet, the deep lines around his amber eyes and beautifully shaped mouth hadn't been there before. And she knew they hadn't been caused by long days spent working in the hot Texas sun.

Seeing those pain-carved lines, and knowing she had put them there, was almost as painful for her as knowing that there was nothing she could do now to make this ordeal any easier for him.

Gabe finally broke the taut silence. He stepped closer to her and lifted his left hand, brushing her cheek with the backs of his fingers. His wedding band was cold against her skin.

"Did you really think," he asked roughly, "there

was anything you could do to yourself that would keep me from knowing you?"

His unexpectedly gentle touch almost dissolved her composure. She flinched away from him, before she could be tempted to do or say anything that would be a terrible mistake—for both of them. "Please don't touch me."

His hand fell to his side. His eyes darkened.

"You needn't worry," he said coolly, moving back. "Neither your life, nor your...virtue is in danger from me. All I want from you is the truth."

She almost flinched at his heavy sarcasm. She concealed her reaction with a lifted chin and narrowed eyes. She kept her mouth stubbornly closed.

His voice roughened with frustration. "Damn it, Page, talk to me. Tell me why the hell you left the way you did."

She'd clamped a mental lid on her emotions now, closing them firmly away. It was a skill she'd perfected over the past thirty months, a talent she'd found indispensable. It had kept her sane.

Emotions weakened her. Distracted her. She could not afford to let them interfere with what she had to do now.

She met his eyes without wavering. "I have nothing to say to you, except that I want you to stay away from me. I want you out of my life."

She'd expected her words to infuriate him. Maybe they'd be enough to make him storm away and never want to see her again.

Instead, he seemed genuinely baffled by her attitude.

"My God," he said in little more than a whisper. "What has happened to you? Who did this to you?"

She didn't allow herself to react to the pain in his voice. In his eyes. She was operating on instinct now, coldly and logically plotting her next move.

"What I am now, or why, is not your concern. I want you to leave me alone."

"You are my *wife*."

She didn't even blink this time. "That was a mistake. One I would have expected you to rectify by now."

He studied her broodingly. "I haven't gotten a divorce."

"You should have. Desertion is sufficient grounds in any state, I would assume."

"Who called you the day you left me?" he demanded, ignoring her comment. "What frightened you so badly that you left without even taking all your things? Why have you insisted on being alone, never making friends or allowing anyone near you? Who are you hiding from?"

She kept her face impassive, concealing her reaction to his questions. She had more than a few of her own.

How had he found her? How much did he know about her actions since she'd left him? How long had he been watching her? Who was helping him?

She asked him nothing. Doing so would only drag this out longer, and she could almost hear a clock ticking in her head.

She had to get as far away from Gabe as possible, as quickly as she could. No matter what she had to do.

"You owe me some answers, Page," he growled when her silence continued. His voice was soft, but dangerous. His eyes focused on her face as though he could see right through the impassive mask she wore.

"This isn't something I want to discuss in my bathrobe," she said, glancing toward the open bathroom door. "You can wait in here while I change."

"And let you climb out a bathroom window? I think not."

She sighed, and spoke condescendingly. "There is no bathroom window. Feel free to check for yourself. But I'm not saying another word until I've dressed."

He looked from her to the bathroom, obviously suspicious. There'd been a time when he had trusted her implicitly, but she wouldn't allow herself to think of those days.

She knew he could see from where he stood that she'd told the truth about the bathroom layout. After a moment he nodded. "Get dressed. But hurry. I've waited long enough for this talk."

She hadn't brought her suitcase in from her car, only her hair dryer, cosmetics case and bathrobe. She picked up the jeans and sweater she'd worn earlier.

"I won't be long," she said as she walked into the bathroom and locked the door behind her.

It didn't take her long to dress. It took her a bit longer to steel herself for what she had to do next. Making sure that mental lid was still firmly locked over her feelings, she slid her hand into the pocket of her jeans and closed her fingers around the slender canister attached to her key ring. Her free hand was perfectly steady when she opened the bathroom door.

Gabe had been pacing. He whirled to face her when she stepped out. "All right," he said. "Now, tell me—"

Her hand came out of her pocket in a swift, fluid movement he never anticipated. Before he could react, she depressed a tiny trigger, sending a thin spray of noxious liquid directly into his amber eyes.

Gabe gave a choked cry, staggered, and covered his face with one hand as he went down to his knees. Coughing from the fumes and cursing the pain, he groped blindly with his free hand, as though reaching out for her. "*Damn* it, Page."

She was already at the door, having snatched her heavy purse from the foot of the bed as she ran past. She spared only a glance back as she jerked the door open.

Just for a moment, the mental lid lifted at the sight of him kneeling in pain. Emotions threatened to spill out of their enforced confinement. "I'm sorry, Gabe," she whispered.

And then she hardened her expression, stepped out of the room and slammed the door closed behind her.

3

GABE GUIDED his pickup into another motel parking lot, pulled into the most isolated space he could find and shut off the engine. And then he waited.

It was after three in the morning. The parking lot was deserted. From Gabe's CD player, which he'd left playing to keep him awake, Larry Gatlin crooned about having "done enough dying today," after the breakup of a longtime relationship. Gabe winced. Country music had both soothed and tormented him these past two years. Sometimes he'd felt as though the songwriters had looked into his own bruised heart.

To distract himself from the sad song, he looked around, spotting Page's car parked at one end of a row of rather disreputable-looking vehicles. This motel was hardly first-class, nor was it in the most prosperous section of Springfield, Missouri.

Page had certainly chosen an out-of-the-way place in which to hide this time, Gabe mused. She hadn't been aware, of course, that she had been followed all the way from Wichita.

He could hardly look at her car without being bombarded by memories of the day they'd bought it. How he'd teased her about checking out the radio before she'd bothered testing the vehicle's performance. The little car still looked pretty good, he noted automatically. No visible dents, though it was dirty. So dirty, he realized, that the numbers on the license plate were almost indecipherable. Accident—or intentional on her part?

Without warning, the passenger door of the truck opened and a man slid inside. He closed the door quickly to shut off the overhead light.

"How are the eyes?" Blake asked, settling comfortably into the passenger seat.

Turning off the music, Gabe scowled and muttered something incomprehensible, trying to ignore the lingering discomfort. It had taken him well over an hour of washing his eyes with water and tears before he'd trusted his ability to drive.

Had Blake not been standing by with his van and his cellular telephone, Page would have made a clean escape. Again.

"You've got to admit the woman's resourceful," Blake commented. After a moment he added, "Something tells me she's had to be."

"Yeah. She's definitely running from something. Or someone. And it isn't me—at least, not entirely," Gabe amended, thinking of her determination to evade him.

"You're still sure of that?"

"I'm sure." He'd been writhing in agony and blind as a bat after she'd zapped him with the vicious spray, but he'd heard her soft apology.

Just as he'd heard the sincere regret behind it.

He was beginning to understand that she had what she considered to be compelling reasons for her actions. But, whatever her motivation, he was still furious with her for what she'd done to him. Everything she'd done to him for the past two and a half years.

"So she's on the run. And she refuses to tell you why."

"Right."

"Has it occurred to you that you have no right to hound her like this? You're basically stalking her, you know."

Gabe shot the other man a savage glance. "I know exactly what I'm doing. I'm trying to put my life back together. *That's* my right."

"How far are you willing to go to get your answers?"

Gabe considered the question—and the somber tone in which it had been asked. What was Blake suggesting? And how far *was* he willing to go?

"As far as I have to," he muttered, as much to himself as to Blake.

Blake nodded in the shadows, as though he'd received the answer he'd expected. "Okay. Then I have a plan."

PAGE DIDN'T SLEEP much that night.

She'd driven as far as she could before exhaustion had claimed her. She'd hoped to get a couple hours' rest and then move on, putting as much distance between herself and Wichita as possible in the next few days, taking a circuitous route that would be difficult, if not impossible, for Gabe to trace. Back roads, switchbacks, obscure towns—Page had learned all there was to know about them. Not that they'd helped her all that much.

She tried to sleep, but every time she closed her eyes, she was haunted by the look in Gabe's eyes just before she'd deliberately sprayed burning liquid into them. It bothered her that she'd been able to do so without the slightest hesitation.

Even though she had to do what she did, shouldn't it have been more difficult for her to have pressed that trigger? How much more damage would she have been willing to inflict to get away from him?

She didn't like the person she had become over the past thirty months. She was beginning to fear that, whatever happened in the future, even if this nightmare were to end, she would never get back the part of herself that she'd had to lock away for her own survival. She was terribly afraid she would never like herself again—and that no one else would, either.

The minutes crept by as she stared blindly at the darkened ceiling.

She didn't try to cheer herself with pleasant memories—memories had become so painful that she'd locked them away with her other vulnerable emotions.

Nor did she indulge in fantasies of a happier future. Hope was something she'd almost abandoned.

Instead, she passed the time visualizing the one constant during this ordeal. The photographs. She could see each one of them in vivid detail in her mind. They flashed through her mind like color slides on a mental screen, replaying over and over, ghostly silent reminders of what she had to do and why.

And she knew that, no matter how much she would dislike doing so, she would hurt Gabe again to keep him away from her.

She simply had no other choice.

GABE STARED out the windshield of Blake's van, keeping watch over Page's room. Blake was stretched out in the back, getting some rest after making the arrangements he and Gabe had agreed upon. It had surprised Gabe how quickly Blake had fallen asleep. The P.I. must have developed the ability to catch some sleep whenever he could.

Gabe wasn't sure he'd have slept even if he allowed himself to try. His thoughts were too disturbing. He couldn't help comparing the cool, unapproachable woman he'd confronted to the sweet young woman he'd married.

He had loved her with an unprecedented intensity that had delighted him at first, and had almost destroyed him after she'd left. Only his grim determination to find her again had kept him going for the past two and a half years.

Now he'd found her. And he'd discovered that she'd become a woman who was almost a stranger to him.

He didn't know what he felt now. Anger was definitely in the forefront. Hurt. Disappointment. Concern, he supposed, about whatever was haunting her.

Love?

Even the word sent a pang through him. He wasn't even sure he was capable of loving that way again.

And yet, would he be hurting this badly if he *didn't* still love her? Why else would he be so devastated by her words, her actions, and most of all, the baffling fear in her eyes when she looked at him?

If nothing else, she owed him an explanation for what she'd done to him. He would remind himself of that every time he questioned whether he had any right to follow through on the plan he and Blake had concocted.

PAGE WAS BLEARY-EYED and groggy when she left her motel room not long after sunrise. Dragging a hand through her unfamiliarly short hair, she unlocked the driver's door of her small car and slid behind the wheel.

She'd showered, but hadn't been able to style her hair, since she'd left her hair dryer in Wichita, along with her cosmetics bag and her favorite bathrobe. She'd dressed for comfort in faded jeans, a short-sleeved blue knit shirt and sneakers.

She didn't think it mattered how she looked today. She planned to spend the day in the car, putting as many miles behind her as possible before she selected the next place she would settle—for a while.

She drove south on Highway 65, thinking she'd

cross the Arkansas state line and then turn east, taking winding rural roads through the Ozark foothills. Maybe she'd head for Tennessee—Knoxville or Gatlinburg, perhaps. Or some little town in between where no one would think to look for her.

She barely got out of Springfield.

Her car engine coughed and her speed began to fall, though she still had her foot pressed on the accelerator. Frowning, she stared down at the gauges.

She'd filled her tank the day before, yet the car acted as though it were out of gas. It coughed again and lurched forward. She clung to the wheel, cursing beneath her breath.

Her trusty little compact had never given her a moment's trouble. Why had it chosen today, of all days, to mutiny?

There was little traffic on the highway at this early hour on a Sunday morning. Nor were there any buildings in sight, only rock bluffs and stubby evergreen trees and highway construction equipment abandoned for the weekend.

"Don't do this to me," she whispered. "Please."

She should have known better than to hope for the best. Her luck just didn't run that way. The engine made one more strangled, gasping sound and died. All she could do was guide the silently coasting car to the shoulder of the road and shift into park.

She beat her fist against the steering wheel. "Damn. Damn, damn, *damn*."

A beat-up truck sped past without slowing. A moment later a family sedan passed. The elderly couple inside it stared at her, but didn't stop. She didn't blame them. They were living in a crazy, dangerous world.

She was walking proof of that.

Walking was exactly what she should be doing, she decided with a sigh. She couldn't sit here indefinitely, waiting for her car to suddenly decide to run again. She had to do something.

Although she knew nothing about engines, she reached beneath the dash and pulled the latch to open the hood. Maybe it would be something obvious even to her, she thought without much hope. A disconnected battery cable or a broken belt or something.

She slid out of the car and walked around to peer under the hood. It was a cool spring morning, and she shivered a bit as she leaned over and peered cautiously at the tangle of machinery. It took her only a moment to decide that whatever was wrong was not something visible to her untrained eyes.

A blue van slowed and pulled over to the side of the road in front of her car. Page tensed as a slender man climbed out and started toward her. His face was shaded by a large black Western hat and mirrored sunglasses. His clothing reinforced the cowboy-wannabe image—a brightly colored, Western-cut shirt and snug-fitting jeans over pointy-toed boots.

He looked innocuous enough, but she no longer accepted anyone at face value.

"Trouble, ma'am?" he asked in a low-pitched drawl.

She nodded, stepping to one side of her car, far

enough away from him to make a run for it, if necessary. "It just died without any warning."

"I know a fair bit about cars. Maybe I can get her goin' for you."

"I'd appreciate it," she murmured, trying to see his face beneath the brim of the hat.

There was something vaguely familiar about him, but nothing she could put a finger on. Yet he seemed more interested in her recalcitrant car engine than in her. He hardly gave her a second glance before ducking beneath the open hood.

She risked taking a step closer. "Can you see anything wrong?"

"Yep. Think I've found it." He reached in and twisted something, grunting with the effort. "Hell. I'm gonna' need my tools. You want to hand 'em to me, ma'am? There's a red toolbox just inside the side door of the van."

Page was becoming wryly amused at his manner. He must be younger than she'd thought at first glance, she decided as she opened the side door of the van. She wasn't even thirty yet and he'd been treating her like an aging aunt.

The van, which looked new, was empty except for a couple of soft drink cans and a small red metal box sitting behind the front passenger seat. Page lifted the toolbox and carried it to the man whose blue-jeaned backside was sticking out from beneath her hood.

"Thanks," he said without looking at her. He set the

toolbox on the car engine, rummaged inside it, and pulled something out.

"I need you to give me a hand here, if you don't mind," he requested over his shoulder.

She moved closer, ducking under the hood. "I don't know anything about cars," she admitted. "What can I do?"

"Hold this wrench," he instructed, guiding her hand to a small silver tool he'd clamped to a connector of some sort. "Don't let it slip, now."

"I won't." She clung tightly to the wrench, hoping she'd be back on the road soon, thanks to this helpful cowboy mechanic.

"Thank ya', ma'am. You've made this real easy for me."

Something sharp jabbed into the soft inside of her outstretched arm. Page yelped in startled pain and let go of the wrench. "What—"

The man's arm went around her waist. She could tell immediately that he was stronger than he'd first appeared. "There's no reason to be afraid. I'm not going to hurt you," he assured her, his Southwestern drawl gone now.

Stunned into immobility, she stared fully into the face beneath the shadow of the Western hat for the first time, and mentally removed the concealing sunglasses.

"Blake," she whispered, a sick feeling gathering in her stomach as she recognized him. "Blake Jones."

"Well, that's half right," he murmured, his arm tightening around her when she began to struggle.

"Settle down, Paula—er, Page. You don't want to fall and hurt yourself."

Her head was spinning, and her vision was beginning to blur. "What did you do to me?" she whispered, the words difficult to force out through her tightened throat. "What are you—"

Her knees buckled.

He supported her gently. "Easy, now."

"I—I—"

Her head lolled. She couldn't find the strength to support it.

He was already leading her swiftly to the van, basically carrying her in his right arm since her feet refused to cooperate. She'd left the side door open when she'd fetched the toolbox for him, so it took him only a moment to place her inside the vehicle.

The slamming of that side door was the last sound she heard before she blacked out on the carpeted floor.

PAGE WOKE with a pounding headache, a nasty taste in her mouth, and a knot of foreboding in the pit of her stomach.

She was lying on her side on a narrow bed in what appeared to be a rustic cabin. The bed, a nightstand, a small dresser, and a straight-backed chair were the only furnishings in the room. There was a window on one wall, but it had been boarded up. The only light came from a small lamp on the dresser.

At least Blake hadn't left her in the dark, she thought

wearily. She tended to be more paranoid than usual when she couldn't see her surroundings.

She rolled onto her back, wincing when the movement made her head throb. She should probably be more afraid, she mused. For all she knew, Blake—or someone he worked for—would be coming in any minute to kill her. Maybe it was a lingering effect of whatever he'd injected into her, but at the moment she was finding it hard to care.

She was tired of running. Tired of being alone and afraid.

Chiding herself for surrendering so easily after all she'd been through, she sighed. Okay, so she'd have to at least make an effort to rescue herself. Even if she had no chance of getting away, she couldn't just lie here and wait for whatever happened.

Gathering all her strength, she sucked in a deep breath and rolled to sit on the side of the bed. She clutched the headboard as the room spun around her. Her stomach lurched and she broke into a cold sweat.

She refused to give in to the nausea. She rested her head in her hands, willing the weakness to pass.

All she needed was a moment, she assured herself. She'd fight this dizziness off, then get up and try the door. She expected to find it locked, but she would make sure. And then she'd see about breaking out.

The bedroom door opened, and she raised her head abruptly. Narrowing her eyes in response to the fresh wave of pain that crashed through her temples, she expected to see Blake enter.

Her heart sank when Gabe Conroy stepped into the room and closed the door behind him.

His eyes searched her face. She knew she looked pale and wretched, her hair limp and straight, her jeans and knit top badly wrinkled.

He, on the other hand, looked wonderful. His long-sleeved, red and white polo shirt clung intriguingly to his broad chest, and his well-worn jeans emphasized his slim waist and strong thighs.

There'd been a time when she'd made every effort to look beautiful for him, she thought with a pang she quickly stifled. She told herself it was better to look weak and vulnerable now. She had to get his guard down if there was any hope of outfoxing him a third time.

"What is it going to take," she asked in a long-suffering tone, "for me to get rid of you?"

A slight twitch in his jaw was his only reaction to her sarcasm. He held a glass of water in his right hand; he offered it to her, along with two small capsules in his left palm. "Blake said you'd wake up with a headache. These should help."

She looked at the pills for a moment, considered refusing them, then nodded and reached out with an eagerness she tried to conceal. She craved relief from her headache, but she was also aware that she needed to be rid of the pain so she could concentrate on getting away from him.

"Thanks," she said after swallowing the pills and

setting the glass on the nightstand. "Now may I leave?"

"Nice **try,**" he said, settling into the chair. He crossed his arms over his chest and stared at her.

She managed to meet his gaze without squirming. "So this is...what? A kidnapping?"

"Something like that."

She lifted an eyebrow. "The Gabe Conroy I remember was an upstanding citizen who would never resort to breaking the law."

A faint flush darkened his cheeks; she suspected it was caused by temper rather than guilt. "Yeah, well, people change," he muttered.

That was something she knew all too well. Gabe wasn't the only one who'd changed. Could she convince him that he wanted nothing to do with the woman she'd become?

"How long are you planning to hold me here?" she demanded.

"As long as it takes," he replied, sounding as stubborn as she was. "I want answers, Page. And I'm willing to do whatever it takes to get them."

He'd obviously intended the warning to intimidate her. She couldn't have explained to him why it made her rather sad, instead.

She was all too aware that there was a high cost involved in being willing to do whatever it took to reach a goal.

She'd been paying the price for two and a half years.

There were times she thought she'd sold her very soul.

4

GABE WISHED he could read Page's expression. She'd looked so wan and ill when he'd stepped into the room that he'd found himself fighting a wave of contrition for what he'd put her through. He'd been on the verge of apologizing when she'd looked him in the eyes, lifted her chin and all but dared him to have sympathy for her.

She was still pale, but it was obvious that her strength was returning rapidly. He could almost see her mind working behind her wary expression, and he'd bet she was waiting for another chance to escape. He was chagrined at how easy he'd made it for her to do so twice before.

She wouldn't find it so easy this time.

"Where are we?" she asked.

"I'm the one asking questions now. You'll have your answers when I've gotten mine."

She sat up very straight, crossed her arms over her chest and looked bored. He could see what the effort cost her.

"You'll let me leave when you've asked your questions?" she asked, her patronizing tone annoying him all over again.

"I think you owe me that much, at least," he returned bitterly, aware that he hadn't exactly answered her.

She seemed to realize the same thing. She looked suspicious, but nodded curtly. "Ask your questions."

"Why did you leave me?"

"I changed my mind about wanting to be married. I hoped to avoid an ugly scene when I told you, so I took off while you were gone. It seemed the easiest way out."

"Who called you just before you left?"

Again there was no hesitation before her answer. "A friend. A *male* friend."

"That's why you decided to leave? You went to another man?"

She didn't blink. "Yes."

Fury surged through him at the very thought of his wife with another man. It was all he could do to keep the emotion out of his voice when he asked, "What happened to him?"

She shrugged. "I got tired of him, too. I'm afraid I have a short attention span where men are concerned."

He focused sharply on her face. Something was definitely fishy about the answers she was giving him. His Page had never been a very good liar—even though she'd improved quite a bit since he'd known her. "Where have you been living during the past two and a half years?"

"Here and there. Sometimes with a man, sometimes

alone. I happened to be alone when your hired gun found me in Des Moines.''

He sprawled back in the chair, appearing to make himself more comfortable. He could tell that his hard-won, laid-back response to her deliberately cruel answers was beginning to get to her. A slight frown had appeared between her eyebrows, belying her nonchalant attitude.

"There've been lots of men since you left me, have there?" he asked, studiedly casual.

She lifted a hand and waved it in the air. "A few. I haven't bothered to count them."

He abruptly switched the line of questioning. "Why did you change your name?"

"There are some unhappy bill collectors looking for Page Shelby. I didn't want to make it easy for them to find me."

He couldn't help but admire her quick mind. She'd yet to even pause before giving him an answer. And he'd bet everything he owned that she had yet to give him an honest one.

"What are you afraid of?" he asked her.

"Nothing," she replied steadily. "Except boredom. Which is what I'm feeling now, by the way. When will this cross-examination end?"

"As far as I'm concerned, it hasn't even begun," he answered. "I'm after the truth. All you've given me so far is a bunch of lies."

He saw her swallow, but she kept her tone impassive. "That's me. A compulsive liar. Might as well write me off as a mistake and let me leave. It's not going to get any better."

"I told you when you could leave. As soon as I'm satisfied with your answers."

For the first time, he saw anger flash through her dark brown eyes. Eyes that he remembered being a clear, honest blue.

"You have no right to hold me here against my will," she snapped.

His own simmering temper boiled. "And I suppose *you* had a right to have me arrested in Des Moines? To try to burn my eyes out in Wichita? Or how about before that? What right did you have to run out on me and leave me to go out of my mind looking for you? Do you have any idea of what you've put me through the past two and a half years?"

"I'm sorry about that. But—"

"'Sorry.'" He shoved himself to his feet with a humorless laugh. "You're *sorry*. Well, that makes it all better, doesn't it, Page?"

She stood, as well. "Haven't you gotten the picture yet? It's over, Gabe. Let me go and get on with your life."

It was obvious that she'd risen too fast. The little color that had returned to her face drained out again.

Gabe caught her arm, steadying her when she swayed. He was standing close enough to catch a faint scent that almost made him groan aloud as old memories assailed him.

Page had changed a great deal since she'd left him, but she still favored strawberry-scented shampoo.

She seemed frozen by his touch, her eyes locked with his, her face strained with more than the aftereffects of Blake's injection.

"One more question," Gabe said without releasing her, his voice hoarse. "Did you ever love me?"

For the first time she looked away before she replied. "No," she whispered. "It was a mistake from the very beginning. I'm sorry."

Her answer—and the pain that shot through him hearing it—infuriated him. He placed both hands on her shoulders, his grip biting into her skin.

"Stop lying to me, damn it!" he almost shouted in her face. "Can't you give me even one honest answer?"

"Yes," she snapped, clutching the front of his shirt in white-knuckled hands. "It's over, Gabe. *That's* an honest answer. Now let me go."

"I can't, Page," he said, hardly recognizing his own voice. "I just can't. Not yet."

He felt her hands tremble as they gripped his shirt. "You can't keep me here," she whispered.

He was puzzled by her expression. She was most definitely afraid, he decided, studying her closely. Her eyes were dilated, her face bleached of color, her breathing rapid and unsteady. "You don't really think I'll hurt you, do you?" he asked.

"You had me kidnapped!"

"You had me arrested," he retorted. "And then you

sprayed liquid fire directly in my eyes. I thought you'd blinded me for life."

"I knew the spray wouldn't cause you permanent harm." She sounded defensive.

"I'm supposed to thank you for your consideration now?"

She sighed and suddenly sagged against him. "This is getting us nowhere," she murmured. "I'm really tired, Gabe. My head hurts and I'm as weak as a kitten. If I could just lie down for a while longer."

He loosened his hands on her shoulders. "Well, I suppose you—"

He'd hardly gotten the words out of his mouth before she sprang into action. Her foot shot out, catching him sharply in the shin at the same moment she shoved hard against his chest. He stumbled. She bolted.

She didn't make it to the door.

Gabe had played a little football in high school. The old moves came back to him as though by instinct when he took her down in a flying tackle. She hit the wood floor with an "oomph," but didn't waste time regaining her breath before she began to struggle.

Kneeling to straddle her, Gabe caught her flailing hands and pinned her to the floor. He was mad enough that he had to make an effort not to hurt her. He would have liked nothing more at that moment than to turn her over his knee. Unfortunately, she would probably bite him in a particularly sensitive area if he tried it.

"Let me *go*," she cried, struggling furiously beneath

him. "Don't you understand that I hate you for doing this to me? I don't love you—I don't love *anyone*. I don't need anyone. I only want to be left alone. Why won't you go away and leave me alone?"

There was an edge of hysteria to her voice. Gabe listened to that, rather than to her fierce words.

With every moment he spent with her, he became more convinced that she was in serious trouble. And regardless of whatever she felt about him now—and whatever he felt for her—he found that he couldn't just let her go.

"Face it, Page. I'm not giving up," he told her, leaning to hold his face very close to hers. "There hasn't been one day since you left me that I haven't searched for you. Do you really think that now that I've found you, I'm just going to let you brush me off with a crock of lies?"

She'd finally gone still, staring up at him with a mixture of anger and desperation. "You can't hold me here forever."

"Once I've gotten my answers, you can have me arrested again," he advised, suddenly weary. "This time you'll have cause. Charge me with whatever you like. Jail couldn't be any worse than the hell you've already put me through."

Her eyes were unnaturally bright, though he didn't see any tears. "It would have been better if we'd never met," she whispered.

Better for her? Or for him? She hadn't specified, and Gabe didn't want to think about it. He had to focus all his energy on the present, on getting the truth out of Page somehow. Something told him it was going to take all his patience and willpower.

"Let me up, Gabe," she said.

He looked at her suspiciously.

She shook her head against the floor. "I won't try to run again. Not yet, anyway," she added candidly. "I haven't eaten since sometime yesterday and I'm still groggy from whatever it was Blake shot me up with. I know I can't get away now."

Gabe was almost amused at her implied warning that she *would* run again, once she had her strength back.

He was still crouched over her, her wrists in his hands, her face inches from his own. He became suddenly aware of the intimacy of their position.

The memories threatened to swamp him, making his body respond. He pushed the emotions ruthlessly aside as he released her more quickly than he'd intended, springing to his feet and backing away from her.

He'd be damned if he'd let his long-deprived body embarrass him in front of her now, when he had the upper hand for the first time—at least temporarily.

"Come into the kitchen," he said gruffly. "I'll make you something to eat."

She stood slowly. He didn't trust himself to offer her a hand. He motioned for her to lead the way out of the bedroom. He was making it clear that he had no intention of turning his back to her.

She glared at him, but turned and stalked to the door. He followed, staying very close, but he was careful not to touch her again.

THE CABIN was an old hunting and fishing retreat a few miles from Table Rock Lake. It hadn't yet been opened for the season, so the windows were still boarded and the furnishings were sparse. While waiting for Blake to arrive with Page, Gabe had made a halfhearted attempt to wipe away some of the dust, but the place could still use a good cleaning and airing.

He hoped they wouldn't be here long enough for that to matter.

Gabe hadn't asked how Blake had found the cabin, nor exactly how he'd managed to get Page here, other than to reassure himself that she hadn't been harmed. He had long since formed the impression that Blake was a good man to have on his side, but would make a formidable enemy.

Gabe wasn't even sure he wanted to know where Blake had developed the skills he'd needed to kidnap Page so competently.

Blake had somehow arranged for the kitchen to be stocked with minimal supplies. Ordering Page to sit at the table, Gabe opened the refrigerator, keeping one wary eye on her. He was relieved when she sat quietly, without appearing to look for a way out.

It was nice while it lasted, he thought wryly, piling food on the counter. He didn't expect her cooperation to last long.

He took a skillet out of a cabinet, and set it on the gas stove. He found a wood-handled knife in a drawer with some mismatched flatware. He used the knife to chop an onion, finding the blade sharper than he'd expected.

The only meat he could find was sliced for sandwiches. He frowned, then started cutting baked ham into cubes, deciding it would do. He didn't have a shredder, so he cut cheese into cubes, as well. He was beating eggs in a bowl when it suddenly occurred to him what he was making. An omelet.

His breath caught in his throat. Page had once loved his omelets. He'd made them for her at least once a week during the short time they'd been together. "The Omelet King," she'd called him—and then she'd always thanked him very fervently for his efforts.

Assaulted by sensual memories of their passionate play, he closed his eyes and tightened his hand around the dented fork. And then he shot a look over his shoulder at Page, who was watching him without expression.

"I guess I should have asked if an omelet's okay with you," he said, his voice gruff.

She nodded coolly. "An omelet is fine."

If she was bothered by nostalgia, she didn't allow him to see it.

Suddenly angry again, Gabe turned back to his cooking.

"There are plates in that cabinet," he said, nodding

toward the door to his immediate right. "Hand me one, will you?"

She rose and opened the cabinet door, pulling down two dusty, brown stoneware plates. Without a word, she rinsed them, dried them with a paper towel and set one beside Gabe, ready for his use.

He concentrating on folding the omelet, and tried not to let the faint scent of strawberry shampoo get to him while she stood so close by. She didn't immediately move away, and he glanced at her out of the corner of his eye.

He went very still.

He'd carelessly left the sharp knife lying on the counter. Page's hand hovered an inch above it.

There was no way he could reach it before she did.

He set the skillet off the heat, turned very slowly and looked her straight in the eye. Her hand remained above the knife, but her face had gone extremely pale.

Staring at him, she moistened her lips.

He lifted a hand to tap his chest, just left of center. "Here's my heart," he said simply. "You might as well finish it off."

A shudder ran through her. She jerked her hand away from the knife and turned toward the table. "Don't burn the omelet," she ordered brusquely. "I'm hungry."

He exhaled very slowly. "I have never burned an omelet," he said, and turned his back to her to finish preparing the meal.

THEY ATE IN SILENCE. Page was aware that Gabe watched her throughout the meal, but she kept her eyes trained on her plate. She was still too shaken to look at him.

She had to get away from him. The thought replayed itself in her mind, building in intensity as her desperation mounted. Every minute she spent with him, she could almost feel danger creeping closer.

She could not allow it to reach them. No matter what she had to do.

The omelet was good. His omelets always were. It was the first omelet she'd had since she'd left Austin.

Memories threatened, but she pushed them back. She couldn't allow herself that weakness now.

Refusing her assistance, Gabe rinsed the dishes and left them in the sink. He poured fresh cups of coffee and nodded toward the living room.

"Let's drink this in there," he said.

In silence and dread of what was to come, she followed him out of the kitchen.

Gabe settled on one end of the lumpy-looking brown plaid couch. Ignoring the space beside him, Page perched on the edge of an uncomfortable burnt-orange armchair.

Watching her over the rim of his cup, Gabe sipped his coffee. She waited for him to question her again, but he remained quiet. Either he knew she would continue to lie, or he was trying to wear down her resistance with this unnerving silence. And it was starting to get to her.

As she watched him drink, the glint of gold on his left hand caught her attention, disturbing her even further. Even though she'd recovered from the original shock of seeing him again, she was still surprised to discover that he hadn't taken the ring off in all this time.

She resisted an urge to lift a hand to the chain at her neck.

She cleared her throat, and the noise sounded unnaturally loud in the quiet room. "Don't you have a business you should be running?" she asked.

He shrugged. "The business can get along without me for a while. I've hired competent foremen to supervise while I take some personal time off."

Foremen. Apparently his fledging construction company had grown since she'd left. There'd been only Gabe and one foreman then. Since Blake was apparently on Gabe's payroll, as well, the company must be turning a profit.

Page wasn't surprised that his business had been successful. Gabe could accomplish anything if he put his mind to it.

That thought, of course, only made her more nervous.

She moistened her lips and tried to think of something else to say. She considered asking about his family, but she didn't want to bring them up now. She'd grown very fond of his mother and sister during the few months she'd known them. Talking about them would only open her up to emotions she couldn't risk showing.

She sipped her coffee and looked at him through her lashes. Her gaze lingered on his left cheek. She remembered the single dimple there that at one time had almost melted her insides every time he'd smiled. She hadn't seen it since he'd found her again.

He looked tired, she thought, studying the dark circles under his eyes, the weary lines around his unsmiling mouth.

"How long has it been since you've had a full night's sleep?" she asked, hardly aware that she'd spoken aloud.

"Two and a half years."

She winced at the blunt reply and looked down at her coffee. She couldn't blame him for the occasional bitter barb.

She didn't blame him for anything, really. In his eyes, she deserved his anger, his resentment, his scorn. She just wished he weren't so darned stubborn. What was it going to take for her to be able to push him completely away from her? What was he hoping to gain by holding her here this way?

"What is it you want from me, Gabe?" she demanded impatiently, setting her mug aside.

"I told you what I want," he replied, apparently unperturbed by her fierce tone. "Answers."

"I've given you answers. You didn't like them."

"I didn't believe them," he corrected her. "I want the truth."

She looked at him with narrowed, suspicious eyes. "And once you've decided I've told the truth—then what? You'll just let me go? Forget about me?"

He took another sip of his coffee. "That depends on what you tell me," he said finally.

"I don't love you," she said, making her tone as cold and blunt as possible.

He didn't react to her statement, except for what might have been a slight twitch at the corner of his mouth. "That's not the answer I'm interested in right now."

"It's all you need to know."

"What are you running from, Page?"

His steady persistence was like water dripping on stone. And she wasn't feeling like the strongest of stones at the moment.

"You," she snapped. "I've been running from you."

"You didn't even know I was looking for you until a few days ago."

He had a point there. She really hadn't expected him to pursue her this relentlessly. Any other man probably would have written her off a long time ago.

But Gabe Conroy wasn't just any man. She'd known that when she married him.

When she'd fallen head over heels in love with him.

She shrugged and managed to speak carelessly. "I figured you would look for me. An ego like yours doesn't take rejection well. You can't imagine that any woman would be immune to your charms."

"I never claimed to be Prince Charming," he returned with what might have been dry amusement.

No, he'd never made such a claim. But there'd been a time when she'd thought he was just that.

The memories were getting too insistent. It was becoming harder for her to keep that mental lid closed. She worried that if she allowed it to open fully, she would never find the strength to slam it down again.

It was the same reason she never allowed herself to cry. She'd been afraid that if she started, she would never stop. She felt very much like crying now. The temptation to dissolve into tears and tell Gabe everything was almost overwhelming.

Only the awareness that doing so could prove deadly gave her the strength to force the emotions aside. Within moments she could feel herself returning to that cool, brittle, ever-vigilant automaton she'd become in the past years. She could look at Gabe without softening now, her mind clear, her thoughts racing ahead, watching for an opportunity to escape.

He lifted an eyebrow as he watched her. Had her mental transformation somehow been visible to him?

"Page?" he asked, sounding wary.

She stood. He did, too.

She took a step closer to him, holding his gaze with her own. "You'll know if I tell you the truth?"

A bit suspiciously, he nodded. "I'll know."

"Good. Then read my lips, Gabe. I want you to stay away from me. *Far* away. Am I telling the truth?"

"Yes," he muttered, looking deeply into her eyes.

"I want you to go back to Austin and get on with your life. I want you to stop following me, stop asking questions that are none of your business. Are those lies, Gabe?"

He shook his head. "No."

She drew a deep breath. "I'm going to leave here now. There's nothing you can do to stop me, short of physically hurting me. I know you won't do that."

"You can't be so sure," he countered, inching closer, their eyes still locked. "You aren't the only one who has changed, Page. I'm prepared to do whatever I think I have to do. Do you believe *that?*"

She searched his face. "Yes," she whispered. "I believe you. But—"

His hands fell on her shoulders. "Give me one more honest answer, and I'll consider letting you go."

She braced herself. "What?"

"Did you love me the day you walked away from me?" he asked unexpectedly.

Her eyelashes twitched, but she didn't look away. "No."

What might have been grim satisfaction crossed his face. "Liar," he said softly.

She caught her breath. "I'm not—"

His mouth covered hers.

His kiss wasn't gentle. It wasn't tender. It held a world of anger and hurt and betrayal.

It broke what was left of her heart.

For only a moment she let herself soften against him.

Her hands rested on his chest, palms spread against his warmth and strength.

The kiss changed. Slowed. Deepened. Just for a little while, she allowed herself to enjoy it.

Gabe was the one who broke away with a deep groan. He buried his face in her hair. "Damn you, Page," he muttered unsteadily.

Her heart spasmed at the pain in his voice. She stiffened and pushed away from him, catching him momentarily off guard. She broke free of him and turned to run toward the door.

Let me go, Gabe. Please, let me go.

Even as she sent the mental plea, she knew it was useless. He wouldn't give up so easily. Not yet.

But still she had to try.

She heard him curse under his breath, knew he was already moving after her. She threw open the door, wondering what the odds were that she could outrun him once she was outside.

She ran straight into Blake's open arms.

She had no trouble recognizing him this time. He'd abandoned the cowboy hat and dark glasses, revealing his thick blond hair and bright blue eyes. He'd changed out of the Western clothing and into a loose white shirt and softly pleated gray slacks. This was the way he'd looked when she'd worked with him in Des Moines.

His hands gripped her forearms tightly, but his smile was deceptively lazy when he looked down at her. "Hello, Page. I have to admit, I wasn't expecting quite such a warm welcome."

Gabe stepped up behind her.

Caught between the two men, Page sighed and pushed a hand through her hair. "Hello, Blake," she said tonelessly. "Won't you come in?"

He chuckled. "Why, yes. I believe I will." He motioned with one hand, still holding her captive with the other. "After you."

"I TAKE IT she's still being uncooperative," Blake remarked to Gabe as they went back into the cabin.

"You could say that," Gabe replied.

Page glared sullenly at both of them.

Blake had been carrying Page's purse and wheeling her suitcase behind him when she'd barreled into him in her futile escape attempt. He'd dropped both to catch her, but he'd retrieved them before coming inside.

He tossed the purse onto the coffee table and set the suitcase on the floor. "I brought these from her car. I thought she might want them. The car's been towed, by the way, and is being repaired. It seems that something foreign got into the gas tank somehow. Gummed everything up pretty badly."

Gabe could see Page's resentment at being spoken about as though she weren't in the room. But he was in no mood to worry about her sensibilities at the moment.

He shouldn't have kissed her, he thought. That had been the biggest mistake he'd made yet.

The kiss had almost unmanned him. For just a moment she'd responded...and he'd been holding his Page again. And he'd known that the old feelings were still there, still alive. Still painful.

"She hasn't told me anything," he said to Blake, trying to think of something besides the all-too-familiar way she'd felt in his arms. "I still don't know why she's been hiding out. Who she's running from—other than me, of course."

Blake ran a hand through his thick blond hair. "Want me to get out the thumbscrews, boss?"

Gabe looked at Page's set expression with a mixture of frustration and bafflement. "If I thought it would work, I just might let you."

Blake shifted his shoulders and slid effortlessly into a James Cagney impersonation. "I can make her talk, boss. Give me five minutes alone with her. She'll be singing like a canary."

Page's eyes snapped with fury. "This isn't funny."

Blake touched her cheek and spoke in his own voice. "No one said it was, sweetheart."

She jerked away from him. "I'm not your sweetheart," she almost snarled. "I'm not anyone's sweetheart."

"We'll debate that later," Gabe said, moving to stand between her and Blake. For some reason he didn't like seeing the other man's hands on Page, even casually.

He motioned toward the chair she'd sat in earlier. "Sit down, Page."

"I'd rather stand."

He took a step closer to her. "I've had just about all I can take," he warned her, speaking very softly. "*Sit down.*"

She sat.

Gabe returned to his seat on one end of the couch. Blake perched on the opposite arm. Both of them looked at Page, who faced them defiantly.

Gabe took a deep breath.

"All right," he said. "Let's put aside personal feelings for the moment. Blake and I think you're in trouble. You've been living the life of a fugitive for the past couple of years. I want to know why."

"You have no right—"

"Page," he cut in, still in that quiet voice he used when he was at the end of his patience. "Don't tell me again what my rights are. You really don't want to get into that with me just now."

She bit her lip and glowered at him.

"Now," he continued. "It's obvious that you're running from something. And, no matter what you may want us to believe, I know damned well it isn't me. We know that you've changed your name at least twice in the past year. Before you moved to Des Moines, you lived in Denver as Pamela Harper."

Her eyes widened. He could tell he'd surprised her with that bit of information, but she didn't speak.

"You worked as a bookkeeper in a mortuary there,"

he added. "Nice, quiet job. Your employer said you were a good worker, but not overly friendly. You kept to yourself. Your landlord said you never had visitors and rarely went out. You wouldn't sign a lease, but paid your rent in advance, always promptly, filed no complaints, caused no problems. And then you moved out two weeks before your rent was due again. You quit your job without notice. Your employer wasn't happy about that."

Page slanted an angry look at Blake. "I suppose your lackey dug that up for you?"

"Lackey? I like that," Blake said, grinning.

"You would," Page said witheringly.

Gabe brought the conversation back on track. "Actually, no. It was the P.I. I used before Blake."

"If I'd been on the case then, you wouldn't have slipped away without anyone knowing about it," Blake murmured.

"Don't bet on it."

Gabe interrupted before the bickering could start again. "A year after you left Dallas, months before we found you in Denver, another investigator identified someone who might have been you who'd lived for a few months in Ft. Wayne, Indiana. She called herself Patricia Webster, a blue-eyed brunette who worked in the claims department of a small insurance company. She made no friends, worked hard and well, then suddenly quit without warning."

Again, Page reacted to the report with a slight grimace. Gabe hadn't known until that moment whether

the woman in Indiana was really Page. At the time he'd
gotten that information, he'd found it hard to believe
she would live under an assumed name, making no effort to contact the people who cared about her.

He believed it now. She really had been on the run.
And he was more determined with each passing moment to find out why.

It was obvious that she wasn't going to volunteer
any explanation. She sat very still, her arms crossed in
a vulnerable, defensive position, her eyes haunted.

Gabe felt another momentary twinge of guilt for
hounding her this way, but he forced it aside.

She was in trouble, he reminded himself. For whatever it was worth, she was still his wife. And he didn't
think either one of them could go on much longer the
way they'd been living for the past two and a half
years.

5

GABE LOOKED at Blake, deciding to try a new tactic. "You've had some experience searching for people who've run away. What are their usual reasons?"

Blake made himself more comfortable on the arm of the couch, looking entirely at ease. He held up one finger. "Running from the law is the primary reason," he said. "Embezzlers, insurance cheats, murderers..."

Page gasped in involuntary indignation, but obstinately pressed her lips together when Gabe and Blake looked her way.

Gabe turned back to Blake. "What else?"

Blake lifted a second finger. "Mental illness. Schizophrenia, paranoia, delusions—all can make a person behave in ways that seem inexplicable. Many homeless people are mentally ill, you know. Or addicted. They're simply incapable of leading what most consider to be a normal life."

Page's scowl grew heavier. Gabe could see she was making an effort to stay quiet in the face of Blake's dramatic speculation.

"I find it rather hard to believe that Page is mentally ill, despite her erratic behavior," Gabe murmured, just a bit tauntingly.

She gave him a withering look. "Thank you for that, anyway," she snapped.

"You're welcome. Blake?"

"Fear," Blake said promptly. "They've done or seen something they shouldn't, and they're afraid of retribution. The witness-protection scenario."

Gabe frowned and swung his head toward Page. That explanation was a more reasonable one, he decided. "Page? Is that it? *Are* you afraid for your life?"

"No," she said, looking him straight in the eye as she answered. "I have no fear for my life."

He was torn between relief and disappointment at the sincerity of her tone. While he was glad that she didn't seem to be in physical danger, at least it would have been an answer he could understand.

"There's another possibility," Blake remarked. "Blackmail."

Gabe was still watching Page; he saw the ripple of unease cross her face in response to the word.

"What on earth could you have done that anyone could blackmail you about?" he asked, perplexed. "And what would anyone hope to gain? You don't have a lot of money, and God knows I didn't when you left me."

She moistened her lips with the tip of her tongue.

The automatic action reminded him forcibly of her sweet taste. He pushed the thought aside, finding it too painful to deal with at the moment. Too distracting.

"Talk to me, Page. Did blackmail have anything to do with you leaving me? And if so, why? Surely you knew even then that there was nothing anyone could have told me that would have changed the way I felt about you."

She seemed to flinch, then to draw more deeply into herself. "I've told you why I left," she said tonelessly. "I made a mistake. I wanted out. I didn't want to be married to you anymore."

Gabe sighed and glanced at Blake, who was watching him for a reaction to her cutting reply. "You see what I've been dealing with?" he asked wearily. "She gives me the same line of bull every time my questions hit too close to home."

"I agree," Blake said with a nod. "She's hiding something. There's more to it than what she's telling you."

"So how am I going to get the truth without her help?"

"You have no right—"

Ignoring Page's angry protest, just as Gabe was doing, Blake considered the question.

"Well," he said. "Looks like you're just going to have to keep digging. If you have no moral objection, you can start by going through her personal things."

Gabe followed Blake's glance toward Page's purse. "I have no objection to that at all," he said flatly.

He reached for the purse just as Page made a lunge for it. "Don't you dare!"

Gabe was faster. He had the purse in his hand before her grasping fingers could close around the strap.

Page jumped to her feet, her face flushed with fury.

"Damn it, Gabe, you can't do this! I can't believe the way you've been treating me. You've been arrogant and overbearing and tyrannical, and that's not the Gabe Conroy I knew. What has happened to that man?"

"*You* happened to him," he snarled. "The Gabe Conroy you knew was a stupid, lovesick fool who naively trusted his wife to honor her marriage vows. He came home one day and found a moronic note in her place. And then he went out of his mind, searching for her, worrying about her, missing her, asking himself over and over what he'd done to drive her away."

Page had gone very still, her face pale, her eyes locked on his face. Blake cleared his throat, looking rather uncomfortable with the painfully personal turn the conversation had suddenly taken.

"*This* Gabe Conroy," Gabe continued evenly, "is tired of hurting, and tired of spending night after night lying awake, wondering what the hell went wrong. This Gabe Conroy is willing to break rules, bend laws, kidnap you, intimidate you, invade your privacy...anything short of physically harming you. I have to know, Page. Now that I've found you, I can't just walk away without the truth."

There was a long, taut moment of silence. Both Gabe and Blake were motionless, looking at Page, waiting for her response. She seemed frozen in indecision, her expression tortured, fine tremors running visibly through her.

"Please, Gabe," she whispered finally, the words

hardly loud enough for him to hear. "You must believe that I know what I'm doing. It would be best for everyone if you were to go back to Austin and forget you ever saw me again. Please. Give me my things and let me go."

He waited a heartbeat, then deliberately opened her purse and dumped the contents onto the coffee table.

Page moved as if to stop him, but Blake cleared his throat in warning. She sighed in angry resignation and returned to her chair, her face expressionless again.

While Blake looked on, Gabe rummaged through the contents of the large leather bag. What he found told him a great deal about the way Page had been living.

Apparently she'd adapted the Boy Scout motto: Be Prepared. She seemed to be prepared for just about anything.

Gabe found a sewing kit, a flashlight, a small first-aid kit, a lighter, and a Swiss army knife with half a dozen functional accessories. There was even another slender spray can like the one she'd used on him. He tossed that to Blake, who stowed it safely in his pocket. Two granola bars. A folding toothbrush and travel-size toothpaste. Travel-size soap and deodorant.

"How the hell did you haul this thing around?" he asked, glancing up at Page. "It must have weighed a ton."

She didn't answer.

Still digging, Gabe found a notepad with an attached ballpoint pen, a solar-powered calculator, a tube of lip balm, a folding comb-and-mirror set, sunglasses and a pair of thick reading glasses. He held those up to his eyes; the glass was clear. The glasses would serve no purpose other than to change her appearance.

He turned the purse inside out to make sure he hadn't overlooked anything of interest.

He found a wallet and a thick, zippered leather pouch concealed at the bottom of the bag. Her driver's license had expired. The address was an apartment in Houston, where she'd lived before Austin. The photograph was more than four years old.

He studied it for a moment, and his throat tightened as the face of the woman he'd married smiled back at him. Clear blue eyes, honey-blond hair. Young and happy-looking.

He couldn't resist glancing at the woman sitting near him now, her face sullen beneath the tousled cap of dark auburn hair, her brown eyes narrowed in resentment. And for only a moment, he allowed himself to grieve again for his lost bride.

He cleared his throat and turned his attention back to the wallet. There were no credit cards or other ID, only two twenty-dollar bills and a handful of change.

And then he unzipped the leather pouch, and he choked. He quickly counted the stack of bills inside, then stared incredulously at Page. "Tell me you don't carry this much money all the time."

She only shrugged and looked away, and he had his answer. Every dollar she'd earned in the various jobs she'd held during the past couple of years apparently went directly into her purse. She hadn't even been willing to commit to a bank account since she'd left him.

"Talk to me, Page," he said again.

She looked down at her lap, where she held her hands in a white-knuckled grip.

He cursed in frustration and opened her suitcase. He found it crammed with clothing, underthings, shoes, sleepwear and toiletries. Nothing superfluous or frivolous—no books, no mementos, nothing that could in any way be construed as sentimental. If she'd had any of those things in her apartment in Des Moines, she'd left them behind.

He almost missed the small, tattered cardboard square stuck in one corner of the suitcase, trapped in the lining. He pulled the card out curiously, feeling as though he'd just made a significant discovery.

"'James K. Pratt,'" he read out loud. "'Detective. Richmond Virginia Police Department.'"

The strangled noise Page made in response to the name sounded very much like anguish.

Gabe brought his head up sharply to look at her. Her expression was still wooden, but her eyes were tortured.

"Who is he?" he demanded.

She turned her head away.

Gabe turned to Blake and held out the card. "Find out," he ordered curtly.

Taking no offense, Blake nodded and slipped the card into his pocket. "Can you hold her here for a while?"

"I'll hold her here if I have to tie her to that chair," Gabe answered flatly. "I'm keeping the batteries charged for my cell phone. Call me when you've got something."

Blake nodded again and pushed himself to his feet. He paused beside Page's chair. "He's not going to give up, you know," he said, his tone surprisingly gentle. "But he only wants to help you. Aren't you getting tired of trying to handle whatever it is by yourself?"

A quiver seemed to run through her, but she remained silent.

Blake sent Gabe a sympathetic look. "I'll be in touch," he said, and then left them alone again.

Gabe was beginning to feel the effects of stress and exhaustion. He tried asking Page a few more questions, but it soon became obvious that she wasn't talking. He decided to stop wasting his energy until Blake provided him with more information.

"I've got to get some sleep," he said, nodding toward the cabin's only bedroom. "Come on."

"I'll wait here," she said, looking rooted to her chair.

"Yeah, sure you will," he agreed sarcastically. "Until I've left the room, anyway."

He held out his hand. "Let's go."

Without touching him, she stood, watching him warily. "What are you going to do?"

"I'm going to make sure you don't go anywhere while I'm resting," he answered, reaching out to set a hand on her shoulder and turn her toward the bedroom door.

She stiffened at his touch, and stumbled when he gave her a slight push toward the bedroom. "I don't suppose you'd take my word that I won't try to escape while you're sleeping."

"I don't suppose I will," he said dryly. "Either walk or be carried, Page."

"I could really hate you for this."

He found her wording interesting, but didn't try to pursue it. "That's just a risk I'll have to take, isn't it?"

With a long-suffering sigh, she finally stopped resisting him and walked the rest of the way into the bedroom without further protest.

He shoved the bed against one wall and nodded toward it. "Lie down."

"You're the one who wants the nap."

He cleared his throat.

She said something beneath her breath he didn't think he wanted to hear. And then she kicked off her shoes and fell heavily onto the bed. At his command, she scooted close to the wall.

He unclipped the cellular phone from his belt and set it on the nightstand. And then he slipped off his shoes and lay beside her, on the outside edge of the bed, his back turned to her.

"I warn you, I've become a very light sleeper," he muttered, settling into the thin pillow. "If you try to get up, I'll know it. And I'll be highly annoyed."

This time he understood her low-voiced response. It was crude and earthy and physically impossible, but for some reason it made him smile. He kept his inappropriate amusement to himself as he closed his eyes and drifted into a light sleep.

PAGE LAY on her back, staring at the cabin's dingy ceiling and asking herself what she'd done in her youth to deserve this sort of pain. She'd always tried to be a good person, to do the right thing. She'd obeyed her parents, followed the rules, made good grades, hadn't smoked or drank or done drugs or been promiscuous.

Her nickname in school had been Mary Poppins, because she'd been so moral and responsible.

And what did she have to show for all those years of clean living? Two and a half years of terror. No family. No friends. No home. No peace.

The only man she'd ever loved lay beside her now, and yet they might as well be in separate states. He was hurt and bitter, and she was too afraid to reach out to him. She still had every intention of getting away from him as soon as possible, even if it meant she had to knock him out and lock him up. And it had to be soon.

She wished he hadn't kissed her.

Her mouth still tingled. Her body throbbed with needs she'd thought long forgotten. And her heart ached with the knowledge that she'd hurt Gabe desperately. And she'd do so again.

She had no other choice.

She had to get away soon, she told herself again. Blake made her nervous. He was much too good at whatever it was he did. It wouldn't be long before he'd have the information about Detective Pratt.

Gabe seemed to have implicit trust in Blake's abilities. For a weak moment Page wished she had Blake on her side. There was a chance that he could help her...

No. That was a gamble she wasn't willing to take.

No one else would die because of her.

She'd learned, to her lifelong regret, that when she made a wrong choice, she wasn't the only one who suffered the consequences. She would cause no more innocent bystanders to pay for her sins. Whatever those sins might have been.

Gabe had been sleeping soundly for a couple of hours. He'd turned in his sleep so that he faced her now, though he hadn't stirred since. His breathing was steady, his lips slightly parted, his muscles relaxed.

She studied him for a moment, thinking that he looked younger in sleep. More the way she'd remembered him on those very rare occasions when she'd allowed herself to think of him.

A lock of brown hair had tumbled onto his forehead. Her fingers itched to brush it back, the way she had so many times in the past.

She curled her hand into a fist to keep herself from making that mistake.

Experimentally, she lifted her head from the pillow. Gabe didn't stir.

Holding her breath, she rose to one elbow, never taking her gaze from his face. When he still didn't move, she tried shifting her weight, inching slowly downward toward the foot of the bed. If she could just slip off without waking him, she could—

His hand shot out to catch her forearm. "Forget it," he growled, his voice gravelly.

She pushed away from him, hoping his reflexes might still be dulled from sleep.

He rolled on top of her, pinning her to the bed with his weight. "You never give up, do you?"

"I was only going to the bathroom," she muttered.

"Be glad your name isn't Pinocchio," he advised, yawning. "As much as you lie, your nose would be ten feet long by now."

"You may get off of me now," she said, clinging to her dignity, despite her embarrassing position.

He didn't move. With his face very close to hers, he took his time studying her. "You look different with brown eyes. But I suppose that was the intention, wasn't it?"

Taking it as a rhetorical question, Page didn't answer. "I can't breathe," she complained instead, pushing futilely against his broad shoulders.

"I've been on top of you in bed before, remember? You never complained then."

She swallowed a groan. Her body was already reminding her of other times when he'd been on top of her—and vice versa. To make it worse, she could tell that his body was remembering, as well.

"Gabe, please," she said, her voice strained. "I'd like to get up."

"It seems that I already have," he commented, shifting his hips against her.

She flushed. "There's no need to be crude."

"Why not? Nothing else has worked so far. Maybe I can embarrass some answers out of you."

"I don't embarrass easily," she said coolly. "Get off of me, Gabe."

He seemed to take the order as a challenge. "I will— when I'm ready."

She curled her lip. "You've resorted to stalking, assault, kidnapping, threats. What's it to be now? Rape?"

She'd hoped to shame him into releasing her. Instead, he cupped her face in one hand, and lowered his mouth to within an inch of hers. "Would it be rape, Page?" he asked in a seductive murmur, his breath caressing her lips. "Would it really?"

Automatically, she moistened her lips. She tried to answer, but her voice stuck in her throat.

Gabe brushed his lips against hers. Lightly. Testingly.

And then he abandoned the taunting and took her mouth in a hard, deep, hungry kiss.

A need greater than her willpower made Page stop fighting him.

Despite her better judgment, she couldn't seem to find the strength to struggle against him just then. Her arms slipped around her husband's neck. Emotions that had been pent up for much too long flooded through her as she abandoned herself to his embrace.

It had been so long since Gabe had held her like this.

GABE COULD ALMOST FEEL his brain empty of thought as he sank more deeply into Page's welcoming softness.

The faint scent of strawberries clouded his mind, and the sweetness of her taste made his entire body pulse with need.

He'd been dreaming for so long of holding her this way again.

He closed his eyes so that he couldn't see the differences in her. He could almost imagine that he was holding his Page again.

The little sound she made when his hand closed over her breast was familiar, as was the ragged cadence of her breathing when he pressed his open mouth to her throat. He remembered every detail as clearly as though it had been only yesterday since he'd last held her.

Hurt, anger and bitterness faded, overshadowed by the heat of passion. Gabe didn't want to acknowledge any feelings beyond desire.

Anything else was simply too painful to contemplate at the moment.

"Page," he muttered, burying his face in her throat. "It's been so damned long."

Her fingers tightened in his hair. Her chest heaved beneath him.

It took him a moment to realize that she was crying.

He lifted his head. She turned her face away, but not before he saw her tormented expression.

Deep sobs racked her. The utter hopelessness of the sounds she made tore at his heart.

"Page, talk to me," he asked one more time.

Her only response was to curl tightly into herself

and cry harder. Gabe suspected that it had been a long time since she'd allowed herself to break down.

He rolled to his side and pulled her into his arms. She resisted for a moment, but then allowed him to press her head into his shoulder. He held her while she cried as though her heart were broken.

His own eyes felt suspiciously damp. Whatever the reasons for her behavior, it was obvious that she was in terrible pain. She felt so slight and vulnerable in his arms. She'd been so very much alone.

For the first time since he'd found her again, he concentrated solely on her feelings instead of his own. And he realized that he wasn't the only one who'd suffered during the past two and a half years.

"Let me help you, Page," he murmured, stroking her hair. "You don't have to be alone any longer. Tell me what's going on so I'll know how to help."

"I can't," she whispered, her breath hitching pitifully. "I can't—I won't take that risk."

"Tell me," he insisted. "Whatever it is, we can deal with it together. You can't go on like this—and neither can I."

He wiped her wet face gently with his hand and gazed into her tear-filled eyes. He held his breath as she parted her lips, looking as though she wanted to speak but was afraid to do so. He willed her to overcome the fear, to finally answer the questions that had been burning inside him for so long.

She cleared her throat. "I—"

Gabe groaned in frustration when the cellular phone

on the nightstand suddenly chirped, shattering the intimacy between them. Page's expression grew shuttered, and she fell silent, looking away from him.

Gabe swung his feet to the floor. He snatched up the phone as it rang again, flipped it open and snapped, "What?"

"Detective James K. Pratt is dead," Blake said without preface. "He died in a rather mysterious car accident sixteen months ago, leaving a young widow and twin toddlers. My sources say he was working a case on his own time, but no one seems to know exactly what it was."

"Pratt's dead." Gabe rubbed a hand over his face as he repeated the news, wondering how many other walls he would slam into before this was all over.

Why had Page been carrying the card of a dead police officer? What did she know about his death, or the case he'd supposedly been investigating?

What the hell was going on with her?

"That's all I've found out so far," Blake concluded. "I'm going to try to get some more details about his last case—unless you need me there?"

"No. Everything's under control here," Gabe lied. "Call me when you find something else."

Gabe closed the phone and turned to Page, who was moving toward the end of the bed again. "Where are you going?"

"I have to wash my face," she mumbled, keeping her tear-streaked cheeks averted from him.

He considered going with her. It irked him that he

still couldn't trust her not to try to escape the moment she was out of his sight. But then he realized that the attached bath had no windows, and the bedroom was still boarded up. She would have to go through the bedroom door to get out of the cabin, and she would find Gabe waiting in the other room.

"All right. But don't take long," he warned.

He could almost feel her resentment of his tone, but she only nodded and headed for the bathroom.

Pushing his unsteady hand through his hair, Gabe went into the living room. He needed to get out of the bedroom, away from that rumpled bed.

He was still cursing the unfortunate timing of Blake's call. If the phone hadn't disturbed them, would Page have told him everything? Or would she have withdrawn from him even without the interruption?

The contents of her purse were still scattered on the couch, and her suitcase lay open on the floor. Though he'd already made a thorough search of each, Gabe felt himself being drawn back to them.

There had to be something he'd missed before.

He found nothing new from her purse, nothing of particular note except the rather large amount of cash in the leather pouch. He set that aside, telling himself he really should find a safe place to stash it for her.

He turned to the suitcase, taking each item out and examining it before setting it aside. Her clothing was unremarkable, made of sensible fabrics and styled for comfort. Her undergarments were plain, serviceable— unlike the filmy bits of lace she'd once worn for him.

His fingers tightened spasmodically around a pair of white cotton panties, and then he threw them aside and continued his search.

He emptied the suitcase, finding not even the vaguest of clues. He searched each pocket, unzipped every zipper. Nothing.

He was just about to give up when he felt the odd lump in the bottom.

It took him only moments after that to discover that Page had created a false lining. He studied it closely and found the hidden closure. With a sense of satisfaction and expectation, he revealed a thick manila envelope that had been hidden within the secret recess she'd devised.

Sitting on his knees on the floor beside the suitcase, he stared for a moment at the envelope in his hands. His first impulse was to rip it open and examine the contents, hoping he would find his answers there.

Something made him hesitate. Maybe it was the conscience he'd been deliberately suppressing for the past few days. The strict code of ethics he'd tried to live by until his search for Page had hardened his heart.

Whatever was in this envelope was obviously intensely personal.

Page's secret.

Did he really have the right to invade her privacy so arrogantly?

He thought of her tears. Her obvious fear. Her broken admission that she couldn't take the risk of unburdening her problems to him.

She needed help, though she wouldn't—or couldn't—ask for it. And he knew of no way to help her if he didn't have all the details.

So, whether he had the right to look or not, he had no other choice.

His hand wasn't quite steady when he opened the clasp on the envelope. "What the—"

The envelope contained photographs. Candid snapshots, grainy and somewhat blurred, taken, apparently, with a long-angle lens, without the knowledge of the subjects.

Most of the shots were of him, Gabe realized to his stunned dismay. And they had been taken over the two and a half years since Page left him.

There was a shot of him on a job site, talking to a foreman. Another of him coming out of a church with his mother and sister—his great-aunt's funeral last year, he remembered.

Another photograph showed him getting out of his pickup in front of the trailer where he and Page had lived together such a short time, and in which he still lived. Some of his friends had tried to talk him into buying or building a house, getting out of the trailer park, but he'd chosen to spend his money on the private investigators who'd been searching for his runaway bride.

He studied a snapshot of himself at a playground with his toddler nephew. His namesake, little Gabriel. And another shot of him coming out of a restaurant with a lovely brunette.

It had been a dinner date his sister had arranged for him, he remembered. Sometime last year. He couldn't recall the woman's name, only that he'd spent the evening regretting his weakness in allowing his sister to talk him into a date he hadn't wanted.

There was another photo of him at a job site. That one, he realized dazedly, had been taken only weeks ago.

Gabe scanned hastily through the other photographs. There were nine or ten of them in all. He didn't recognize the subjects, though the same faces appeared in a couple of them. A smiling young man with a woman and two small children. A pretty, chubby blond carrying a baby. The same blond walking down a sidewalk, pushing a carriage and holding the hand of a round-faced little boy. A heavyset woman in jeans and a University of Iowa sweatshirt stood outside what appeared to be the apartment building where Gabe had found Page in Des Moines.

His eyes were drawn back to the shots of himself. Who the hell had taken them? And why?

A cracking sound from the other room brought his attention abruptly back to the present.

Page had been in there quite a while, he realized suddenly. And now he had a whole new batch of questions to ask her.

Clutching the photos, he frowned in grim determination and headed for the bedroom. This time, he vowed to himself, he wasn't letting her get away with her lies.

PAGE FIGURED it was her last chance to escape, though the odds were stacked against her. Keeping one eye on the open bedroom door, she stood by a window that couldn't be seen from the other room. As quietly as possible, she'd slid the window open and was now working at removing the thin sheet of plywood that covered the opening from the outside.

Unlike Blake, Gabe wasn't the most adept of kidnappers, she thought wryly. Lack of experience, probably. Though he'd managed to get her here—thanks, in part, to her own stupidity—he'd left her with her jeans, top and shoes. And he hadn't searched her clothing. She'd been relieved to find the slender, nearly flat penknife still hidden in the lining of her right sneaker. She'd carried it by habit, finding it occasionally useful...now, for instance.

She pried carefully at the thin sheet of wood. It had apparently been hastily tacked into place, more to provide protection for the glass panes than to guard against break-ins. It certainly wouldn't have kept out a determined intruder—and Page hoped it wouldn't keep her "in," either.

She held her breath as she felt the board give a little. A sense of urgency gripped her. She had so little time.

Gabe was getting too close to the truth, and she didn't want to think what he would do if he learned the whole story. He tended to overreact, she thought, wryly considering her present situation. But taking on her problems could prove more dangerous than he ever imagined.

The board loosened further, but this time with a creaking sound that made her cringe and look nervously at the door.

Time ticked swiftly away from her, making her next actions critical. Should she continue to move slowly, trying to be silent, or simply shove the board away from the window and make a dash for freedom?

She heard Gabe moving around in the other room and knew her time was almost out. Taking a deep breath, she slammed both hands against the wood and pushed against it with all her strength.

The board fell away with a loud crack, revealing a thick stand of woods and a cloudy gray sky outside. Page dove through the open window. She hit the rocky ground and rolled instantly to her feet.

She heard Gabe call her name, but she was already running. If she could lose herself in the woods, hide somewhere until she had another chance to run again...

Some deep, logical part of her mind knew her actions were irrational. She knew Gabe would never let her get away this easily. But she had to try. The emotions that had overwhelmed her when she'd cried in Gabe's arms were driving her now, urging her on, haunting her with the high price of failure.

Hearing Gabe close behind her, she sprinted and dodged among the budding hardwoods and scraggly evergreens, her heart pounding, her vision clouded with tears and fear. She stumbled over the uneven ground, but kept her footing. If only—

Gabe's hands fell on her shoulders, jerking her abruptly to a stop. She strained against him, but he turned her roughly around.

His face was flushed with anger, and his amber eyes snapped fire. He was breathing harshly, and the lines around his eyes and mouth had deepened, emphasizing his fierce scowl.

"Why do you keep doing this?" he bellowed, giving her a shake that spoke as much of frustration as anger. "What the hell are you trying to do to me?"

"I'm trying to keep you alive!" Page shouted, her control finally gone. "I will not have another man die because of me. Don't you understand that I would rather die myself than have anything happen to you?"

6

STANDING IN THE WOODS outside the little cabin, Gabe stared into Page's distraught face, trying to comprehend her words. "What are you talking about?"

She'd gone so pale he thought she might faint. He tightened his grip on her shoulders.

Her eyes were huge. Wild. Glittering with barely suppressed emotions and unshed tears.

And they were blue. Bright, summer-sky blue. Apparently she'd removed her appearance-altering brown contacts while washing up from her bout of tears.

She tried to avert her face. He caught her chin in his hand and turned her to look at him again. He was shaken by the sudden reappearance of the woman he'd married. "Page—"

Still half hysterical, she shoved against him. "Let me go! You have to get away from me, don't you understand? As long as you're close to me, your life is in danger. I won't be responsible for another family's grief."

He held on to her, easily overcoming her efforts to break away. "Who died because of you?"

"Detective Jim Pratt," she whispered, her expression haunted. "He was only thirty-two. He had a wife and two children. And now they're alone—because of me. All because of me," she finished, sobbing.

Gabe thought of what Blake had told him about Detective Pratt.

Detective James K. Pratt is dead... He died in a rather mysterious car accident sixteen months ago, leaving a young widow and twin toddlers... He was working a case on his own time, but no one seems to know exactly what it was.

"What did you have to do with Pratt's death?"

"He died because of me," she repeated, and grief dulled her voice. "Because he was trying to help me."

"You're saying he was murdered?" Gabe couldn't quite keep the skepticism out of his own voice.

She gripped his shirt in her hands. "Yes! He *was* murdered. Just as anyone else who gets close to me will be. Including you."

Gabe shook his head, slowly, wanting to understand, half afraid to believe. "Why?"

Her breath caught. "I don't know," she whispered as her hands went slack. "I don't know why. I only know that it's true. And I won't take the risk of losing anyone else I care about. If I have to live alone in a cave, or if I have to take my own life to save yours, I'll do it." She finished with a renewed determination that unnerved him.

He took one hand from her shoulder to shove it through his hair. "This is insane."

"Yes." She seemed to have no argument with that assessment, at least.

His head was beginning to hurt. Another dull ache began somewhere in the middle of his chest.

"You're trying to tell me you walked out on me to *protect* me?" he asked incredulously.

She swallowed hard and nodded. "I was afraid to stay." The words were barely audible. "I couldn't take the chance..."

"And you thought that was best for me? To come home and find my wife missing? To suffer the hell I've been through ever since? I went to the police when you disappeared. I begged them to help me find you. They took one look at the note you left and wrote you off as a runaway wife. I think half of them were convinced I'd killed you and concocted the story to cover up my crime. I've put my life on hold for two and a half years looking for you, spending every penny I had on private investigators. No one found any reason to believe you've been in danger."

He wasn't sure which came through stronger—hurt, anger or disbelief. None of this made sense to him. Nothing she'd told him sounded remotely credible.

And yet, Detective James Pratt was dead. And there were those photographs...

"I did it for you," Page murmured. "I would have done anything to keep you safe."

"You never considered letting me make the decisions about my own safety?" he asked bitterly. "You could have told me whatever was going on, given me a chance to work it out with you."

"I couldn't take the risk." She seemed to have withdrawn from him emotionally, retreating deep inside herself. Away from his anger, his pain—perhaps away from her own.

"This is crazy," he snapped. "Nothing has happened to me. I have no reason at all to believe you."

"No? What about that accident on the bakery job?" she challenged.

He frowned, the words stirring memories of an incident he hadn't thought of in years—since Page had left him, to be precise. "You mean the beam that fell at the job site a couple of years ago?"

She nodded. "It missed you by inches. Your crew said you'd been within a hair of being killed."

Gabe remembered now. The mishap had taken place a few days before Page left. Shaken, but unharmed, he'd told her about it, figuring that someone else would if he didn't.

She'd been very upset, he recalled. She'd cried at the thought of how closely she'd come to losing him—and then she'd made passionate love to him for hours to reassure herself that he was safe.

They hadn't spoken of the accident again after that night. Gabe had assumed she'd put it out of her mind. He'd never imagined the incident had anything to do with her leaving.

"I remember," he said slowly. "But—"

"It wasn't an accident. It was a warning. To me."

"From whom?"

She sighed, as though exasperated by his obtuseness. "I...don't...know," she said, speaking as though to a slow child.

Gabe thought suddenly of Blake's half-serious speculation that Page was mentally ill. Gabe hadn't wanted to believe it—and neither had Blake—but now he was beginning to wonder. Was she suffering from delusions? Paranoia? Did her bizarre behavior indicate that she had totally lost touch with reality?

Page was watching his face, her eyes sad. "You don't believe me."

He thought of Detective Pratt's suspicious death. The photographs in Page's suitcase. She hadn't taken the most recent one of him—he had proof that she'd been in Des Moines when it was snapped. So who *had* taken it? And why did Page have it hidden in her bag?

Frustration welled inside him. He was tired, hungry and confused. He hadn't eaten anything since the omelet he'd prepared some nine hours earlier, and now evening was creeping through the woods, scattering ominous shadows among the dense trees. Page jumped and looked around nervously when a night bird suddenly called from close by. She acted as though she fully expected an attack at any moment.

"I think we'd better go back inside," he said wearily. "I want you to start from the beginning."

Looking as though she'd rather commit hara-kiri, Page nodded, her eyes downcast.

"And by the way..." Gabe added conversationally, keeping one hand firmly on her arm. "If you try to run again, I'm tying you to that chair. Is that clear?"

She gave him a resentful look in answer.

Satisfied that he'd made his point, Gabe led her to the cabin.

GABE DIRECTED Page to sit on the couch, and then he reached for the photographs he'd dropped haphazardly when he'd realized what she was doing in the bedroom earlier. He tossed them onto the coffee table in front of her. "I assume these have something to do with this wild tale you've been telling me?"

She glanced at the photos, and then quickly away, as though she couldn't bear to look at them for long. "Yes."

He crossed his arms over his chest. "All right. From the beginning."

She frowned. "Must you loom over me? Sit down."

Though tempted to remind her that she was in no position to be snapping orders, he pulled one of the armchairs closer to the couch and settled onto it. "I'm sitting. Now talk."

She combed her fingers through her tousled auburn hair and drew a deep breath. It still rattled him to see the blue eyes he'd remembered so clearly looking back at him. As long as she'd worn the dark contacts, he could almost convince himself that she wasn't his Page, but a near stranger. A woman who couldn't hurt him the way his wife had.

Now, except for her hair color, she looked very much as she had when he'd first fallen in love with her. And it was eating him alive.

"Two days before that beam almost hit you," Page said quietly, "I received a phone call. I'd just gotten home from school, and you weren't due home for another hour or so. I didn't recognize the man's voice, and he wouldn't give me his name. But he called me by mine."

"What did he say?"

He saw her swallow. "He said I shouldn't have married you," she answered unsteadily. "He said I'd made a very big mistake. He said I didn't deserve a family and that he was going to make sure I would be as alone as he was."

"You never told me about it." It still hurt him to realize she'd kept so much from him.

She shook her head. "I assumed it was just a crank call. I hung up on him, and he didn't call back, so I thought it was over. I was going to tell you, but—well, you came home in such a good mood. It was our two-week anniversary and you brought me candy. You were still feeling guilty because there wasn't time or money for a real honeymoon—not that I cared about that. We were so happy. I didn't want to ruin our evening."

Her words were like slivers of glass in his heart. He remembered that night. Remembered how young and besotted he'd been, how foolishly smug about his marriage to the woman he adored.

"It was our three-week anniversary the day you left me," he murmured, hardly aware that he spoke aloud. "I brought you flowers then."

She flinched. "I'm—"

She stopped and cleared her throat, then took another deep, unsteady breath. "When I got home from work the day I...I left, I got the mail as usual. There was an envelope addressed to Page Shelby Conroy. No return address. When I opened the envelope, I found two photographs. Nothing more."

She leaned forward and plucked two photos from the stack, pushing them toward Gabe. One of them was of the woman holding a baby. The other was of Gabe on a job site. "Those are the ones," she said.

Gabe pushed his emotions aside and studied the photos, trying to concentrate on the unfolding story. "Who is she?" he asked, motioning toward the woman with the baby.

"Jessie Carpenter. She was a very close friend of mine from college in Alabama—the only one who supported me during the ordeal there that I told you about. She's holding her youngest child, Amelia, who was born a couple of months before I met you. Jessie sent me pictures when Amelia was born, but I couldn't understand why this one was enclosed with a snapshot of you."

"You didn't connect it to the telephone call?"

"Not immediately. Mrs. Dooley came over just then to give us a loaf of her bread. She and I talked for a few minutes, and then the phone rang. I answered it, and she motioned that she had to go. She left just as I realized the caller was the same man who'd called before."

"What did he say?"

"When I realized who it was, I was going to hang up again, but then he said something about your near-miss at the bakery job. He said it hadn't been an accident. He told me he'd been responsible for that beam falling and that he could just as easily have killed you with it."

"That beam fell because a piece of equipment broke," Gabe protested.

She stubbornly shook her head. "He said it was his work. And then he asked me if I'd gotten the photographs. When I said I had, he told me that my friend had two sweet young children. He said something about how vulnerable children are. How easy it is to harm them."

Gabe felt a cold chill slither through him. He began to understand how horrified Page must have been by the mysterious, cold-blooded threats.

She cleared her throat and twisted her fingers in her lap. "I asked him what he wanted. He said again that he wanted me to be alone, as he was. He said I had to leave you, or you would die. He said if I told you about the call, or tried to stop him, I would pay—by losing you."

"So you ran."

She looked him in the eyes. "I ran," she said simply.

He wanted to shout at her, to demand again to know what right she'd had to make that decision for him. With an effort, he restrained the resentment. "Where did you go?"

"I just started driving. A couple of days later I was

sitting in a hotel room in Nashville, Tennessee. I wanted to call you then. I knew you must be upset—"

"Upset," he murmured tonelessly, wondering if she had any idea how little resemblance the word bore to his actual reaction.

She darted him a nervous glance and continued. "I had my hand on the telephone to call you when it rang. It was him—again. He asked how it felt to be alone. He told me I'd made the right decision—that I'd been within twenty-four hours of becoming a grieving widow. He told me he'd know if I tried to contact you or the police. And that he would make sure someone I loved would pay for my mistake."

"He followed you from Austin to Nashville?"

"Apparently. I was so frightened by then that I almost believed he knew my every action—my every thought. I begged him to tell me why he was doing this, what I'd done to him. Who he was. He only warned me again not to get close to anyone. And then he hung up."

"And you changed your mind about calling me," Gabe said with regret.

"I dialed the number," she whispered. "You answered, sounding so distraught and anxious that it broke my heart. But then I pictured you being hurt or...or worse, because of me—and I couldn't handle it. I hung up."

"Damn it, Page." He breathed the words through emotion-clenched teeth. "You should have told me."

She closed her eyes. "I was too afraid. I loved you so

much. There was nothing I wouldn't do to keep you safe."

Had she loved him? He couldn't help but ask himself the painful question. He could accept that she'd felt responsible, frightened, confused...but could she have walked out of his life that way if she'd *really* loved him?

Unable to respond to her statement, he went on with his gruff interrogation. "You had no idea who the guy was?"

"None," she answered, spreading her hands. "As far as I knew, I didn't have an enemy in the world. The only man who'd ever had cause to resent me was dead. I couldn't think of anyone else who would do this to me."

"What did you do then?"

"I kept moving. I tried to make sure I wasn't being followed, but of course I had no experience in that area. I ended up in Bowling Green, Kentucky. I was running out of money, so I found a job as a stockroom clerk, where my public contact was minimal. I used a false name. I thought it would make it harder for him to find me. I found an inexpensive apartment where I wasn't required to sign a lease. I thought I could hide there until I decided what to do next. I had a telephone with an unlisted number installed so I could call the police if...well, if someone tried to break in. At the time, I thought there was some chance that my own life could be in jeopardy."

"Go on," he said when she paused.

She'd gone colorless. "I was so lonely. So desperately unhappy. I found a stray kitten on my way home from work one evening, and I took him in, craving the companionship. He..." Her voice broke.

Gabe leaned automatically closer to her. "What happened?"

She seemed to gather her courage. "I came home one evening, unlocked the front door, and...and found the kitten in my kitchen. Dead."

She swallowed audibly. "The phone started ringing almost immediately. I knew who it was, of course. I didn't want to answer, but I was afraid not to. He said I shouldn't have gotten the kitten. I was to have no companionship in my life. No love. Not even a pet. He added that he could just as easily kill a person as a cat, so I should picture you or Jessie's children dying like my kitten if I dared disobey him again."

Gabe almost reached out to touch her. He resisted the urge with some difficulty.

He couldn't afford for either of them to be distracted again now, not while she was finally talking. "I'm sorry, Page."

She nodded. "I called the kitten Buddy," she murmured inconsequentially. "He was very sweet."

She drew a deep breath. "I couldn't stay there after that, of course. I...cleaned up the mess in the kitchen, so there would be no reason for anyone to be suspicious of my leaving, and then I turned in my key to the landlord. I gave him a phony story about my father being ill, and I left. I stopped on a country road to bury

Buddy beneath a big tree. I couldn't just throw him in a Dumpster like a piece of garbage."

Gabe wondered what else she'd buried in that roadside grave. Hope? Courage? The lighthearted spirit of the happy woman she'd been before?

She continued without being prompted. "I went back on the road. I spent a few weeks in Joliet, Illinois, a month in New York City. I met Detective Pratt in Richmond, Virginia, one evening when I had a flat on the side of a highway. He helped me change the tire, and then he gave me a searching look, handed me his card and told me to call him if I ever needed help again."

Gabe could feel his tension building. Page's voice was emotionless now, but her eyes…her eyes spoke of a woman in torment. She hardly moved as she spoke. Her chin was high, her shoulders squared, her hands locked in her lap. She had the air of someone bravely facing a firing squad.

"You called him?" he asked.

"I called him. It was two days later. I'd been waiting tables at a grubby little diner for ten hours and I was exhausted. I was sitting in a dump of an apartment, alone, tired, depressed, hopeless. I went out for a walk and I found myself standing at a pay phone, Detective Pratt's card in my hand. I thought of you, and of Jessie and her children. I prayed that I wasn't making a mistake you would all have to pay for. And then I dialed his number."

She jumped suddenly to her feet. Startled, Gabe stood, too, ready to block her if she tried to bolt.

"I'm thirsty," she said. "I have to have a drink."

He motioned toward the kitchen. He was right on her heels when she turned and walked to the fridge. He wasn't letting her out of his sight again.

The fulminating glance she shot over her shoulder told him she knew what he was thinking and resented it, but he ignored it. Impatience simmered through him. It was all he could do to restrain his questions until Page had rummaged through the fridge and pulled out a soft drink. She closed the refrigerator door without waiting to see if he wanted anything.

"What did you tell Detective Pratt?" he demanded as soon as she'd taken a long swallow. "What did *he* say? What happened to him?"

Page turned to look out the window over the sink, though Gabe suspected that she wasn't really seeing the moon-washed scenery outside.

"He wasn't very old. Early thirties," she murmured. "Your age. He had a warm smile and an infectious laugh. He had a wife and twin children he loved dearly. I'm sure they miss him desperately."

Her voice had thickened. She cleared it before she continued. "We met at a coffee shop close to my apartment. He bought me coffee and listened to my story without saying a word. I was sure he thought I was just another nutcase with a wild tale created for attention. He didn't. He believed me."

She took another sip of her drink, still staring blindly

out the window. "He asked me to let him call you, so you would know that I was all right. It was just over six months after I'd left Austin, and he suggested that you would still be sick with worry. He thought we should warn you that there was reason to be concerned about your own safety. I almost agreed—but then I pictured Buddy's poor, mangled little body and I begged Jim not to involve you. The caller had told me you were safe as long as I stayed away from you, and I felt I had no choice but to believe him. Jim didn't fully approve. He said if I were his wife, he'd want to know everything, whatever the risk, but he accepted my decision."

"I had a right to know the truth."

She shrugged, as though silently pointing out that they'd been over this already. And then she went on. "He promised to help me. He was afraid there wasn't enough evidence to convince his superiors, since all I had were a few relatively innocent-looking snapshots and an improbable-sounding story He said he would work the case on his own time until he came up with something more concrete. I don't know what he did after that. Made some calls, I suppose. Dug around in my past, trying to find something...anything...to provide a clue."

She set the cola can on the counter and looked at Gabe with tear-filled eyes. "A week to the day after I called him, he was dead."

7

GABE LAID a gentle hand on Page's shoulder. "Why don't you sit down?"

She allowed him to guide her to the table, where she sat stiffly in a chair, her eyes staring into a painful past.

"What happened to Detective Pratt?" Gabe asked, keeping his voice low.

"I came home from work one evening and found an envelope that had been slid beneath my door. There was only one photograph inside. It was Jim Pratt— with his wife and children."

Gabe remembered the shot of the happy-looking young man with a woman and twin toddlers. Detective James K. Pratt and family.

"I panicked," Page whispered. "I rushed to a pay phone and called the police station. I had to warn him that he was in danger...that the man stalking me had somehow discovered that Jim was helping me. They...they told me..." She choked.

Gabe reached across the table to cover her icy hand with his own. "What were you told?"

"I learned that Detective Pratt had died the evening before in a car accident. Half in shock, I bought a newspaper, and read that the accident had happened under very strange circumstances. There was evidence that he'd been deliberately forced off a very steep curve, though there'd been no witnesses. The chief of police was calling for an investigation, but I...I knew they wouldn't find anything. I knew Jim had died because of me. Because he'd wanted to help me. I killed him when I made that call," she whispered.

Gabe's fingers tightened around hers. "That's ridiculous," he said roughly. "Even if this lunatic *did* kill Pratt, you can't blame yourself. It wasn't your fault."

"James Pratt died because of me," Page insisted. "His wife and children and parents and siblings grieved at his graveside...because of me."

She caught her breath on a sob and forced words out. "I couldn't deal with it. I ran. When I couldn't drive any longer, I got a motel room. I don't even know what town it was in. I took a sleeping pill and fell into bed, still in my clothes. I didn't want to think. The phone rang in the middle of the night, waking me."

Gabe didn't have to ask who was calling. "He told you he'd killed Pratt?"

"He was furious. He told me he'd almost gone after everyone else who had ever mattered to me. You. Your family. Jessie and her children. All of you. He told me if I ever went to the police again, I was signing your death warrants. He said he'd start with the children— because they'd be easy. He told me he might be taken out along the way, but not before he'd gotten to someone I loved. Someone else who wouldn't deserve to die."

She swallowed another sip of her drink, her hand unsteady as she lifted the can to her pale mouth. The cola seemed to burn its way down her throat, judging from the face she made.

"I begged him to leave you all alone," she said after a moment. "I asked him to kill me, instead. He knew where to find me. It would be so easy. He only laughed—an ugly, vicious laugh. He had no intention of killing me, he said."

"And?"

"I told him I would kill myself," she whispered. "I told him I'd rather die than have him hurt anyone else because of me. I told him he'd left me nothing to live for, anyway. I was fully prepared to do it that night."

Gabe felt a cold rush of horror go through him. It was caused by the look in her eyes, the tone of her voice. He believed absolutely that she'd been prepared to go through with her threat. To end her own life.

"He wouldn't have liked that," he said, imagining the man's reaction to the threat of having his victim permanently removed from his sick games.

"He started screaming at me. Cursing me. He said if I dared take the easy way out—the self-serving way out, he called it—everyone I'd ever cared about would die, as well. And he would be angry enough when he killed them that he would make sure they suffered."

"He's insane."

Page snorted with a spurt of the spirit she'd subdued since she'd begun her tale. "What was your first clue?"

"And you have absolutely no idea who he is?"

They'd been over that question before, but Gabe was still finding it hard to believe someone could hate her that much without her even suspecting who it was.

"I don't know," she repeated flatly. Believably. "If I did, I would tell you. I've told you everything else."

"Everything?"

She shrugged. "You know the rest of the story. I've kept moving, changing identities, cities, finding work when I ran out of money, doing my best to keep from endangering anyone else along the way. I lied, of course, when I told you I'd been with other men. There were no men. No friends, no lovers, no one. I tried so hard not to let anyone get close enough to be endangered just by being near me."

Rubbing a weary hand over her face, she said, "Everywhere I went, he found me, no matter how well I thought I'd covered my tracks. Sometimes it took him a few weeks or months, but there was always a day when an envelope arrived in the mail or beneath my door."

She moistened her lips. "The day you found me, in Des Moines, I had just received two more photos. One of you. One of the woman who managed the apartments where I was living. I hadn't befriended her, but I liked her. She was kind to me, no matter how often I rebuffed her friendly gestures. Her kindness had put her in danger. I knew I had to run again, to protect her."

"And you ran straight into me."

She groaned. "Yes. I was horrified to see you. I knew

if he found out you were near me, that you had entered my life again, he'd..."

She couldn't finish that sentence.

"He always finds out," she whispered. "He's the devil, and he can't be stopped."

Her eyes turned wild again, her voice frantic. "Gabe, please. Let me go. Get away from me—as far as you can. I couldn't bear it if anything happened to you."

He was a bit shaken by her passionate plea, but he shook his head. "If you're asking me again to go home and forget about you, don't. I won't do it."

She made a strangled sound—half sob, half growl—and shook her hand free of his. "Don't you understand?" she shouted. "This man is a murderer! And you will be his next victim if you don't do what I ask."

"Not if we find him first."

From her reaction, he might as well have suggested they sprout wings and fly to safety.

"It's too dangerous," she whispered. "He's too good at this."

"He's a man, Page, whatever exaggerated delusions you've concocted over the past couple of years. He can be stopped."

Shaking her head, she stood and backed away from the table, her hands raised in a gesture of pleading. "I...we can't. He'll kill you, Gabe. Or if not you, another innocent bystander. He has no conscience, no mercy. He doesn't care what he has to do, as long as it makes me suffer."

Gabe almost asked her why she would suffer if he

were killed. Because she couldn't stand the guilt of another death on her behalf? Because she'd once cared for him enough to marry him?

He knew now that her reason for leaving him had been noble, at least in her own mind. Maybe she really had convinced herself she'd had no other choice, that the sacrifices she'd made had been necessary. Selfless. Maybe some people would consider her a martyr to love, a heroine of epic proportions.

Gabe was still hurting too much to see her in that light. As much as he had loved her—as much as he suspected he still loved her—it still hurt him that she hadn't come to him the moment her problems had begun. That she'd run without a word of explanation to him.

She hadn't given him a chance to help her. To help them both. She hadn't trusted him to take care of himself, or her. And that lack of faith slashed at some deep, primitive male part of him that had expected his wife to turn to him for protection. To see him as her champion, strong and fearless and invulnerable.

Instead, she'd seen him as a helpless target. A victim. And she'd taken it upon herself to leave him alone, groping cluelessly for answers, blaming himself for her desertion.

She hadn't believed in him then. He would damned well make her trust him now...even if he died trying.

"I'm calling Blake," he announced in sudden decision. "He seems to have a great deal of experience that could prove helpful to us now."

"You'll just be endangering him, too." There was desperation on her face now, mingled with resignation. She'd finally accepted that he wasn't going anywhere until this mess was resolved—one way or another.

"I'll tell him everything. Give him the chance to decide for himself whether he wants to stay involved. That's more than you gave me," he added with a bitterness he didn't try to conceal.

She flinched as if he'd struck her. "I thought I had no other choice," she whispered.

He stood and turned his back to her. Now wasn't the time to get into "should haves" or "would haves." First, they'd see about tracking the demented killer Page claimed was after them. Then they would decide what to do about their marriage.

PAGE STOOD for a long time in the middle of the kitchen, hardly able to breathe.

Gabe hated her. Even after hearing the whole story, after she'd told him she'd acted out of love for him, he was still bitter and angry that she'd left without an explanation.

She thought of all she'd done for him, all she'd sacrificed to keep him safe. Her home. A job she'd loved. Companionship. Security. She'd tossed it all away. For him. Because she loved him. She always had. Always would.

And he hated her for it.

For the first time since he'd brought her here, he'd

left her alone in a room with a door to the outside. She heard the low murmur of his voice in the other room, knew he was occupied on the telephone, telling her story to Blake. She looked longingly at the kitchen door.

She could run. And this time, she might even get away. For a little while.

But Gabe would follow. She understood that fully now. He wasn't going to let her walk away again. He would keep following her until he found her...or until the stalker killed him for daring to get close to her. And there wasn't a damned thing she could do to stop him.

Suddenly overcome with exhaustion and despair, she sank into her chair and buried her face in her hands. She couldn't run any more. At least now, with Blake on his side, Gabe had a fighting chance. He'd finally been given his choice, and he'd decided to stay with her until it was over. She didn't try to tell herself he stayed out of love.

No, this time Gabe intended to be the one to walk away...when he was good and ready, and not before.

She only prayed that he would live long enough to have the satisfaction of leaving her.

THE WOOD-HANDLED kitchen knife, a four-pronged fork and a dented spoon danced through the air as if they had a life of their own. Up and over, around and across. Dancing, spinning, falling. Page found herself half mesmerized by their movements, her mind numbed by fear, weariness, heartache and despair.

Blake seemed to pay little attention to the sharp instruments he juggled so casually. Leaning against the kitchen counter, he'd started juggling them almost absently as he listened to Gabe repeat the story Page had told him. He wore pearl-gray slacks with a soft, pale-blue shirt and he looked more like a handsome lounge performer than the clever detective Page knew him to be.

Blake glanced at Page. Seeing her staring at his busy hands, he stopped his juggling and nodded toward the barely touched burger she held loosely in front of her on the table. "Eat," he prodded gently. "You must be hungry."

She wasn't, actually, but she forced herself to take a small bite of the rapidly cooling burger. Blake had brought fast food when he'd arrived, and Gabe had managed to consume his dinner while he'd talked. It was all Page could do to choke a few morsels past the lump of fear in her throat.

Blake looked at the penknife lying on the table, close to Gabe. The knife Gabe had taken from her outside.

"If you're going to carry a knife, Page," Blake commented, "you need one a bit more effective than that puny little thing." He grinned and lifted one leg of his loose-fitting slacks, exposing a leather knife case strapped to his ankle. His knife was anything but a "puny little thing."

She swallowed and looked away, uncertain whether he'd been trying to reassure her as to her safety or intimidate her into cooperating with him and Gabe.

Blake frowned when Page suddenly set her burger aside, her appetite completely gone now, but he didn't insist that she eat it. Instead, he began to question her, just as Gabe had earlier. "You have no idea why anyone would do this to you?"

"None," she answered tightly, her patience strained. "I only know that this man has killed once—twice, if you count my kitten—and that he's willing to do it again. He has an uncanny ability to find me wherever I go, and to get within photographing range of people I care about."

Even empty, Blake's hands seemed restless as he plucked at the crease in his slacks, picked a minuscule dot of lint from his shirt sleeve, straightened his collar. "No jilted lovers?" he asked. "Ex-boyfriends who had reason to resent your marriage to Gabe?"

Feeling her cheeks warm, she shook her head. "No ex-lovers," she muttered. "I...didn't date much in school. My parents were very strict when I was in high school, and I was rather shy and studious in college. I concentrated on my schoolwork, and had very little social life."

Something made her glance at Gabe. She found him watching her with an expression that made a shiver of reaction run through her.

Gabe could have told Blake that there had been no jealous ex-lovers. Page had been a virgin when she met Gabe—something she'd shyly told him on their fourth date. He'd been almost primitively pleased by the idea, and quixotically old-fashioned enough to insist that they wait until their wedding night to consummate their relationship.

And then he'd insisted impatiently that they be married very quickly.

Their wedding night had been perfection.

"The professor who harassed you in college," Blake continued, apparently unaware of the new tension that had developed between Page and Gabe. "Could this possibly have anything to do with him?"

Forcing the memories away, and hoping her cheeks weren't as red as they felt, Page turned her attention back to the P.I. "Gabe told you about that?"

Gabe shook his head. "He found out on his own."

"Professor Wingate is dead," Page said flatly. "He shot himself, his wife and his only child four years ago, over a year after he was fired by the university where he'd taught for more than twenty years."

"Because of your charges against him," Blake murmured.

"Yes," she said, glaring at him. "I suppose you could say that he, too, died because of me."

"That's not what he meant, Page," Gabe said.

"No, it's not," Blake agreed. He looked at her with a sympathy she didn't want to acknowledge, because it frightened her too much to consider that she was no longer alone, no longer without friends.

She couldn't afford to let her guard down after all this time. For Gabe's sake, for Blake's—for her own.

She nodded curtly. "Whatever. He'd dead. He couldn't possibly be behind this."

Blake tugged at his lower lip. "Tell me about him."

She grimaced, reluctant to rehash the sordid debacle. "He was a computer science professor, nearly forty years my senior. I took his class the first semester of my final year, needing one more credit toward my degree. I don't know why, but sometime during that semester, he...well, he seemed to become obsessed with me," she said uncomfortably.

"He started asking me to stay after class, ostensibly to discuss my work, but treating me in a way that made me uneasy. He asked me out. I knew he was married, and I turned him down—which I would have done even if he had been single. He started writing me notes. Love letters. Calling me. Following me around the campus."

"Had he ever done anything like that before?" Blake asked.

"Not that I know of. No one wanted to believe me when I told other students what was going on. He was eccentric, even a bit weird, but he seemed to genuinely like his job. He was a popular instructor, and his students didn't want to hear anything negative about him. I tried to deal with it without turning him in. I dropped the class before the semester ended. He didn't give up. I finally had to go to the dean. I took the letters and a message left on my answering machine to prove my claim."

"They fired him immediately?" Gabe asked.

Page shook her head. "They warned him to stay away from me. He'd never done anything like that before, and he promised it wouldn't happen again. Two days after our meeting with the university administrators, he started calling me again. Begging me to run away with him. Telling me he would...he would kill himself if he couldn't have me."

"What did you do?" Blake asked, when Gabe only growled something beneath his breath.

"I went back to the dean," she replied, rubbing her forearms against a sudden chill in the room. "I asked for his help. That's when Professor Wingate was fired. It was a deal he made with me and the administrators. We all agreed to keep the matter as quiet as possible, on the condition that he never contact me again. He took early retirement, kept his reputation relatively intact, his legal record clean—and I was able to finish my last semester of college and earn my degree in peace."

"Did his wife ever learn about you?" Blake wanted to know.

Page winced. "I'm afraid so. She called me, the day after he was fired. She asked me to recant my story. She told me he loved his job, and wouldn't be able to survive without it. She...she told me she was sure I'd misunderstood. She said he loved her deeply, and would never leave her for anyone else. I felt so sorry for her, but I told her there was nothing I could do. I asked her to please not call me again, and I hung up."

She could still hear the woman's sobs, haunting her. Making her wonder if there hadn't been some other way to have handled the mess.

But Page had been so young, and had no experience

in dealing with anything like that. Her parents were both dead, and she'd had no one else to turn to during the ordeal, except her young friend, Jessie. She'd just wanted to be left alone.

"A couple of years later, after I earned my graduate degree in Houston, I received a congratulatory note from a friend in Alabama. She mentioned in the letter that Professor Wingate had shot himself and his family. My friend thought I already knew, but I hadn't heard, since I'd deliberately distanced myself from that whole experience. I was upset, but I convinced myself it wasn't my fault. Even if Professor Wingate's suicidal depression developed when he was fired, there was nothing else I could have done at the time."

"There's no way anyone could consider it your fault." Gabe sounded as though he would hear no argument.

Blake didn't seem as certain. "You said the caller told you he didn't want you to have a family. That he wanted you to be alone, as he was. Wingate shot himself, his wife, and a son. You're sure there was no surviving offspring?"

"From what I know, there was only the one son. He would have been in his late teens when he was killed. I was told that the boy walked in on the scene just after his mother had been killed, and that Wingate then shot his son before turning the gun on himself."

She shuddered, trying not to imagine the gruesome incident. The terror and betrayal the boy must have felt in those last frightful moments.

"There has to be a connection," Blake muttered, still lost in thought. "A man kills his entire family because of you, and now someone else wants you to suffer. To be alone. It's too much of a coincidence to overlook."

Page almost felt her cheeks blanch in response to Blake's careless wording. *Because of you.*

Professor Wingate had lost his job. Because of her.

Wingate, his wife, and his son were dead. Possibly because of her.

James K. Pratt was dead. Because of her.

Gabe was in danger. As were Jessie and her children. And now, very likely, so was Blake.

Because of her.

"It's not your fault, Page," Gabe said, staring at her with narrowed eyes, as though he could read her thoughts. "You had no control over Wingate's actions, and you can't take responsibility for this lunatic who's been stalking you. The only mistake you've made was to run away without giving me a chance to help you."

She knew he meant the words to comfort her. He probably wasn't aware of the accusation laced beneath them. She bit her lip.

Blake glanced sharply from Gabe to Page. His expression softened. "You believed you had no other choice," he said, and it wasn't a question.

Page felt her eyes moisten. Blake understood, she thought.

Why couldn't Gabe see that she had left him, not because she hadn't loved him, but because she'd loved him more than anything else in her life?

Gabe stood abruptly. "I'll get the photographs," he said, moving toward the doorway. "You can look them over, Blake, and see if there's anything you can learn from them."

"Good idea," Blake said.

Page remained silent.

Without looking at her again, Gabe left the room.

"You can't blame him for being hurt," Blake said softly when he and Page were alone. "I know you've been through a difficult time the past couple of years, but he has, too."

"I know," she whispered.

"Do you really?" Blake didn't look convinced. "Everyone he knows thinks his wife deserted him three weeks after the wedding. He wasn't joking when he said there was some suspicion that he had harmed you. I heard a few rumors to that effect."

She caught her breath. "No one who really knows Gabe could believe anything like that of him."

"I have a feeling he's changed since you left," Blake murmured. "He has gained the reputation of being a hard man. Driven. Cold. He lets his guard down only with his immediate family. And even they say he's not the same man he was before."

Page frowned. "You interviewed his family?"

"I wanted to make sure he hadn't killed his wife and hired me to cover his tracks."

Page caught her breath at Blake's phlegmatic statement. "That's a horrible thing to say!"

Blake shrugged. "He wouldn't be the first who'd tried to dupe me."

Page would bet that few had succeeded. Something about Blake made her uncomfortable, even as it reassured her to have him on her side.

Hearing Gabe moving around in the living room, Page looked a bit wistfully in that direction. "He hates me now," she murmured, hardly aware that she'd spoken aloud.

Blake's expression gave little clue to his thoughts. "Is that what you believe?"

She swallowed painfully. "I see it in his eyes when he looks at me."

"Then maybe you'd better look again."

Blake straightened, and pushed a hand through his heavy fall of blond hair. "Gabe's not the only one who has changed during the past couple of years," he said. "Could be he's in there asking himself what you feel about *him* now."

She bit her lip. She didn't want to examine her feelings for Gabe too closely. It hurt too badly to consider that the giddy, desperate, all-consuming love she'd once felt for him might no longer be returned.

As she'd discovered during the past two and a half years, there were times when it was infinitely more comfortable to feel nothing at all.

BLAKE DIDN'T STAY long after he'd examined the photos. He seemed to think the best plan of action would be for Gabe and Page to stay safely hidden at the cabin while he dug more deeply into the Wingate murder-suicide case. He still believed, he told them, that there had to be a connection between that incident and Page's tormentor.

"I'll stay in touch," he told Gabe as he took his leave, tapping the cell phone clipped to his belt. "You keep your guard up."

Gabe nodded. "I will."

Page couldn't help wondering if they were referring to her or the lunatic who'd been stalking her. She suspected that Gabe was almost equally wary of both of them.

Blake turned to Page before stepping out into the night. "Get some rest, blue eyes," he murmured, touching the worry line between her eyebrows with the tip of one finger. "You aren't alone in this anymore."

A pang shot through her heart. He had no idea, she was sure, of how much his words meant to her. Or how badly they frightened her.

"Be careful, Blake," she whispered.

He flashed her a high-voltage grin. "Careful is my middle name," he assured her.

It occurred to her then that she didn't even know his last name—at least his *real* last name. He was gone before she could ask him.

She turned to Gabe and saw that his face was dark, his eyebrows drawn into a fierce scowl.

"Blake is on my payroll," he said curtly. "That's the only reason he's involved with this."

She lifted her chin, stung by his tone. If he was warning her not to take Blake's interest personally, he needn't have bothered. She'd spent two and a half years distancing herself from others. She would not change that habit now—not until she was absolutely certain that anyone she called a friend would not be automatically targeted by a madman.

And didn't Gabe understand that friendship was all she could ever offer any other man except him? Gabe was the only man she'd ever truly loved. She had been willing to give up her life for him, despite his doubts. Nothing had changed—not her feelings, nor her determination to keep him from harm, whatever she had to do.

"I hope you're paying him well," was all she said to Gabe, forcing her voice to sound as cool as his. "You've just put his life at risk. Something tells me that's not what he had in mind when he took this case."

8

THE CABIN seemed almost unbearably quiet after Blake's departure. Page and Gabe sat in the living room, trying not to stare at each other. Page thought she would go crazy if one of them didn't say something soon.

She cleared her throat. "I don't suppose Blake will have any new information before morning."

His expression rather brooding, Gabe shook his head. "No. Probably not."

"Should you call your family? Let them know you're all right?"

Again, he shook his head. "I've told them I'll be out of town for a few days. That's all they need to know for now."

Page plucked at a string that dangled from the hem of her top. "How *is* your family?" she asked, giving in to the curiosity that had been building inside her.

"They're fine. Mother fell just before Christmas and sprained her back, which kept her down for a while, but she seems much better now."

"How awful for her. As active as she is, she must have hated being laid up."

He glanced at her, as though wondering whether she

really cared about his mother's discomfort or was just making conversation. "Yes. She did."

He didn't seem inclined to continue the conversation, but Page persisted, needing to fill the silence between them. She nodded toward the stack of photographs Gabe had replaced on the coffee table after Blake had examined them. "The picture of you and Gabriel at the park—I couldn't believe how much he's grown. He looks very much like you."

"That's what my mother and my sister both say. Curt sort of resents it," Gabe said, grudgingly responding to her efforts as he mentioned his brother-in-law.

Page had been especially fond of Gabe's only sister during the brief time she'd known his family. "Is Annie still working for Dr. Shewmaker?"

He nodded. "She still seems happy running his office."

"Good for her. I've...I've missed them all."

The look he shot her made her bite her lip. "They missed you, too," he said. "I wasn't the only one you hurt when you took off."

She flinched.

He sighed. "Sorry," he muttered. "I guess I'm on sensory overload right now. A lot has happened today."

She nodded. They fell silent again.

Gabe finally shoved a hand through his hair and cleared his throat. "We're both dead on our feet," he said, making her struggle to suppress a wince at his unfortunate wording. "Let's get some rest. You take the bed. I'll sleep on the couch."

She didn't question the sleeping assignments. Nor did she argue. "Fine."

"I'm going out to nail that plywood back into place over the window. You can have first shot at the bathroom."

Page glared at him. "It isn't necessary to nail me back into the bedroom. I'm not going anywhere."

There was really no point in trying to escape tonight. She had no idea where they were, and Gabe would just follow her, anyway. She knew when to bide her time.

He sighed impatiently. "I'm not nailing you into the bedroom. Obviously, that didn't work before. I'm simply covering the glass again. I'd just as soon not have anyone peering into the windows without our knowledge."

She shivered. "That's a pleasant thought."

"Yeah, well, this situation has me thinking that way."

A few minutes later she heard him moving around outside, using the full moon for illumination as he hammered at the plywood with what sounded like a large rock hitting the nails still stuck in the board. She rubbed her hands over her face, dreading the next few hours.

Alone all night in a cabin with a man who was legally her husband. A man she'd once given her heart and her body to with equal abandon. A man who looked at her now as though he could hardly stand to be in the same room with her.

She took a deep, unsteady breath, and reminded herself that she'd locked the hurt away with those other feelings that were too intense for her to handle now. And then she headed for the bathroom to get ready for bed.

She didn't wear a nightie, but a large black T-shirt over a pair of gray sweatpants, with white tube socks. Hardly sexy sleeping attire—but she wasn't trying to seduce anyone. She was only interested in being ready to run at a moment's notice, if necessary.

Or so she told herself.

She was in bed by the time Gabe came back into the cabin. He'd taken his time outside. Had he been patrolling the premises for signs of danger? Or trying to avoid being alone inside with her for as long as possible?

Either way, she decided she didn't really want to know.

He went into the bathroom without looking at her as she lay in the darkened bedroom. The door closed with a snap. Lying on her side, idly fingering the chain around her throat, she stared blindly at nothing, and listened to his movements. She heard the shower running, and pictured him stripping off his clothes and stepping beneath the water.

She gulped and squeezed her eyes shut, trying to close out the disturbing image. It didn't help. The picture stayed in her mind with unsettling clarity.

She told herself she was suddenly hot because the cabin was stuffy with all the doors and windows closed. There was no air-conditioning, no fan to move the air. She didn't want to believe her sudden heat had anything to do with the mental image of Gabe lathering himself with soap.

She ached. Until Gabe had held her while she'd cried a few hours earlier, it had been two and a half years since she'd allowed herself human contact. She'd almost forgotten how nice it felt to be touched. Hugged. Stroked.

Loved.

And, oh, God, it hurt.

This was exactly what her stalker wanted, she reminded herself despairingly. He wanted her to be achingly aware of her solitude. He wanted her to crave companionship with a need that bordered physical pain. He wanted her to know exactly how it felt to be totally alone, even when surrounded by others. He would be delighted to know how much she was suffering now.

What had she done to him to deserve this?

"Page?"

She jumped at the unexpected sound of Gabe's voice from the shadows. "What?"

"You okay?"

She wondered if she'd made some sound in her misery. "I'm fine," she said.

"I'll be on the couch, if you need me."

She nodded against the pillows, then remembered

that he couldn't see her clearly in the darkness. "All right."

"G'night."

"Good night, Gabe."

He hesitated in the doorway a moment longer, as though there was something else he wanted to say, and then he turned and moved away. Page slowly let out the unsteady breath she'd been holding.

THOUGH SHE HADN'T expected to, Page slept awhile. She woke with a dry mouth and the feeling that her dreams had been disturbing, though she couldn't remember the details. There was no clock in the bedroom, but she'd left her watch on the nightstand. She groped for it, and pushed the button to illuminate the dial.

Three a.m. Monday, she remembered.

It was hard to believe it had been Saturday morning when Gabe had found her in Des Moines. So much had happened in such a short time.

She was still tired, but she didn't expect to go immediately back to sleep. She needed a drink of water. She wondered if she would be able to slip into the kitchen without waking Gabe.

Telling herself she shouldn't risk it, she rolled onto her back and tried to sleep. But her thirst wouldn't be ignored. The room seemed to get stuffier, her mouth drier. Finally she sighed, tossed the sheet aside and swung her legs over the side of the bed.

Her socks made no sound on the hardwood floor as

she tiptoed across the room to the open doorway. Gabe had apparently left a light on in the kitchen. Keeping her eyes fixed on that welcome glimmer, she made her way carefully past the couch where he lay, his breathing deep and even.

The dim light over the stove was burning when she entered the kitchen. She was glad Gabe had thought to leave it on. It provided all the illumination she needed to find a plastic tumbler in the cabinet and fill it with water from the tap. She tipped the glass back and drained it gratefully.

There was a tiny window over the sink, a round piece of glass that resembled a ship's porthole. The owner hadn't bothered to board that one, and Page stood for a moment gazing out at the moonlight-silvered woods.

She saw no other lights, no evidence of any civilization near the little cabin. She was torn between optimism that the stalker would never find them in such an isolated place, and fear that there would be no one to help them if he did.

"What are you doing?"

The husky growl caught her unprepared. Page gasped and whirled, stumbling against the countertop, the plastic tumbler falling from her hand to clatter against the linoleum floor.

"It's just me," Gabe said, stepping into the soft light to reveal an expanse of hard bare chest above the cotton gym shorts that was all he wore. "Chill out."

She had a hand pressed over her racing heart. She

glared at him, annoyed at his casual attitude about scaring her half out of her wits. She tried to ignore how very good he looked, his tanned skin gleaming in the soft light, his coffee-brown hair tousled from sleep, his amber eyes heavy and glittering.

"I didn't hear you get up," she said.

"I thought you might be trying to leave again."

"I was getting a drink," she said haughtily. "I told you I wouldn't try to leave."

"Yeah, well, I tend to be a bit skeptical about your promises these days."

The words stung. She crossed her arms defensively over her chest, and swallowed the automatic protest that sprang to her lips.

Gabe grimaced and shoved a hand through his hair. "Look, I'm sorry," he muttered. "That wasn't necessary."

"No. It wasn't."

"I'm just tired, I guess."

She nodded stiffly. "I'll let you get back to sleep, then. I'm sorry I disturbed you."

She moved toward the doorway, intending to breeze past him, but he remained where he was, blocking her path.

Looking at him uncertainly, she paused. "Was there something else?"

He started to speak, then closed his mouth and shook his head. "No. I guess not."

He moved aside.

She tingled all over as she passed within touching

distance of all that bare male skin. She kept her hands carefully at her sides.

He followed her to the bedroom. "Page?"

She laced her fingers in front of her and turned toward him. He stood in the doorway, silhouetted against the faint light from the kitchen. She couldn't see his face, and she doubted that he could make out her expression, either. "Yes?"

"How long were you going to keep running? How did you think this would end?"

"I don't know." She spoke softly, but her voice seemed to echo in the silent shadows. "I told myself I would run as long as I had to. Maybe I was foolishly hoping he would come to his senses one day and leave me alone. I haven't had much time to think or to plan during the past thirty months, only to react."

"You never considered calling me? Asking for my help?"

The hurt was still there, in his voice. The sense of betrayal. Of wounded male pride.

"We've been over this, Gabe. I was afraid to involve you."

"You thought I was so incapable of taking care of myself? Of you?"

"I didn't want to take the chance. I couldn't risk your life," she repeated stubbornly.

"Damn it, Page." His voice was raw. "You keep saying you left me to save my life. Didn't you ever stop to think that without you I *had* no life?"

She caught her breath. "I'd been on my own for a

long time," she tried to explain, wishing there was something she could say to soothe his pain. "I was used to being alone, to dealing with my own problems. But you—you had your family. Your friends. Your business. I was in your life such a short time. I—"

His curse was vicious. Earthy. Unexpected.

"You are my *wife*," he said, his voice strained. "Three weeks, three years—or thirty—it wouldn't have mattered. Everything changed for me when I married you. We were supposed to be a team," he finished bitterly.

She closed her eyes, swaying slightly on her feet. "I know. I wanted that, too. But he came so close to killing you with that falling beam. I was so afraid..."

She opened her eyes, willing him to understand. "There were so many times I wanted to call you. So many times I wanted to tell you everything. To beg you to forgive me. But when he killed Buddy—my kitten— I realized how cruel he could be. And when he killed poor Detective Pratt, a trained police officer, I knew he wouldn't hesitate to go after you."

Her breath caught. "I didn't want to leave you, Gabe. It was the hardest thing I've ever done in my entire life. The past two years have been sheer hell for me, but I've gotten through them because I believed I was doing the best thing for you. I told myself if I had to spend the rest of my life on the run, it would be worth it, because no one could ever take away my memories of the twelve perfect weeks I'd had with you."

She didn't add that she hadn't even allowed herself

to savor those memories during the time she'd been away from him. It had simply hurt too much to remember.

"And you really thought *I* could forget those weeks?" he asked, sounding incredulous. "Just put our marriage behind me and go back to the way things were before I met you? You honestly thought my feelings were that shallow?"

"I— No..."

Had she thought it would be so easy for him? Had she had so little faith in the love he'd claimed for her that she'd thought he could put it behind him and go on as if he'd never met her?

She still remembered how amazed she'd been when Gabe Conroy, the handsome, virile, dashing young man she'd fallen in love with almost at first sight, had told her he'd felt the same way about her.

She'd been shy and inexperienced and awed by the intensity of her feelings for Gabe. She'd fallen in love for the first time in her life. She'd been literally swept off her feet by Gabe's passionate, whirlwind courtship—but had she failed to comprehend how much it had truly meant to him?

"I'm so very sorry I hurt you, Gabe," she murmured. "If there had been any other way..."

He sighed wearily. "There *was* another way, Page. You could have told me."

"I wouldn't risk your life," she repeated. How many times had she already told him that? How many more times would it take before he believed that she'd had no other choice?

"Why can't you understand," she asked, "that I loved you enough to give up everything for you?"

"And why can't you understand," he asked roughly, "that we should have faced this together? I know you'd been accustomed to handling everything on your own before we met, but when you married me that was supposed to have changed. We married for better or worse, remember?"

"Until death do us part," she whispered with a shiver. "And that was an ending I just wasn't ready to face."

"We keep coming back to the same place," he muttered, sounding discouraged. "You say you're sorry, but you still won't admit that you were wrong to leave."

She swallowed a huge lump in her throat. "I couldn't let him hurt you," she whispered.

"And yet *you* almost destroyed me," he answered starkly.

Another sob ripped through her. "I'm— Oh, God, Gabe, I only wanted—"

Before she'd even realized he'd moved, he had her in his arms. He held her in a desperate, almost painful grip, his face buried in her hair. She felt the fine tremors running through him, and she clung to him, offering comfort, seeking something she was afraid to define.

His skin was so warm. She'd almost forgotten how

the muscles rippled beneath the surface, how the coarseness of hair contrasted so deliciously with the sleekness of flesh. She could feel his heart hammering in his chest. His erection swelling against her abdomen.

He still smelled faintly of soap and shampoo from his quick shower. Nestling against him, she closed her eyes and indulged herself in experiencing him with her other senses.

His mouth moved against her cheek, and then closed over hers. Page lost herself in the kiss.

She'd been alone for so long. For so long, she'd dreamed of him holding her like this, comforting her, sheltering her from the pain, the fear.

A groan rumbled deep in Gabe's throat, making his chest vibrate against her breasts. He worked his hands beneath her loose T-shirt to stroke her bare back. His palms were warm against her skin—hot. Greedy. He slid one hand lower to pull her more snugly against him.

He wanted her. She had no doubt of that. He made no effort to hide the evidence. But was there more? He'd loved her once—did he still? Were the old feelings still there, buried somewhere beneath the hurt and the pain?

"Page," he said, his voice raspy. Shaken. "I—"

She pulled back to look at him, straining to see him in the darkness. She saw only the feverish glitter of his eyes. The hunger. The need.

A need that seemed to match her own.

She placed her hand gently against the rock-hard line of his jaw. For the first time in so very long, they were together. Alone. They had this one night.

If nothing else, she thought wistfully, maybe she'd been given a chance to properly say goodbye to him. A chance that she had been too afraid to take before.

"I've missed you, Gabe. I've missed you so badly." She ran a fingertip over his mouth, and felt his lower lip quiver beneath her touch. She remembered the first time he'd kissed her. How she'd known even then that her life would never be the same.

She heard him swallow, saw the new tension that gripped him. She rested her hands on his shoulders and leaned into him, remembering the first time he'd held her. She'd been so struck by his size, his strength, the warmth that had radiated from him. She remembered wishing that she could stay forever within the safe circle of those strong arms.

"I've missed you," he admitted, his voice hoarse. "Sometimes I thought I would go insane..."

"Will you come to bed with me, Gabe?" she asked, and it took all her courage to say the words. "Will you make love with me?"

If only one last time, she added silently, refusing to allow herself to hope beyond this night.

He went rigid against her, as though fighting emotions that flooded through him in response to her request. She didn't know whether he'd won or lost the inner battle when he gathered her into his arms and moved toward the bed without speaking.

She'd thought they would make love in the darkness. Gabe lay her on the bed and reached out to snap on the bedside lamp.

"I've been dreaming about this for too damned long," Gabe muttered in answer to the question in her eyes. "This time I need to know it's real."

She blinked away a sudden film of tears and held out her arms to him.

He swept the gray fleece pants down her legs and tossed them aside, got rid of the socks, then reached for the hem of her black T-shirt. Blushing, but willing, she helped him, leaving her clad only in cotton panties and a thin gold chain.

Gabe froze, staring at the small gold ring that dangled from that chain.

The ring that matched the one he still wore on his left hand. The ring he had bought for her, and had placed on her finger as he'd vowed to love her for the rest of his life.

His hand closed unsteadily around the ring. "You're wearing this wrong."

She moistened her lips. "I know."

He slid the chain over her head, removed the ring and lifted her left hand. She was trembling when he pushed the band onto her finger, his gaze holding hers captive. He tossed the gold chain carelessly onto the nightstand.

He didn't give her a chance to say anything—not that she would have known what to say if he had. He took her into his arms and crushed her mouth beneath his.

Gabe seemed determined to relearn every inch of her, as though comparing reality to the memory he'd carried of her. He tasted her throat, nuzzled behind her ears, nibbled at her shoulders, lingered at her breasts until her toes curled into the sheets and her fingers clenched spasmodically in his hair. He nipped at her tummy, stroked her thighs, tickled behind her knees, kissed her toes.

And then he removed her panties and devoted his attentions to other, more intimate areas.

Page was shuddering, gasping, aching with a hunger that threatened to consume her from the inside out. How many nights had she fantasized about this? About being with Gabe again, holding him, loving him. Being loved in return.

"Gabe," she managed to plead, her voice hardly recognizable. "Gabe, please."

His face was darkly flushed, his eyes glinting with near-feral desire. "I'm trying to make this last," he grated. "It's been so damned long, I'm ready to explode."

She looked at him uncertainly. Surely he didn't mean...?

"There's been no one else," he said, uncannily reading her thoughts again. "You should know by now that I didn't take my marriage vows lightly."

She was finally beginning to understand exactly how seriously Gabe *had* taken those vows. Seriously enough to search for her for two and a half years. Seriously enough to spend who-knew-how-much on private investigators. Enough to put his personal life on hold until he found her again. Enough to risk his very safety now to help her out of the mess she'd somehow gotten into.

She was both awed and dismayed by the depth of his commitment. She could see now that she'd underestimated the passionate young man she'd married.

She'd learned the hard way not to do so with the stubborn, angry, determined man he'd become.

For the first time, she wondered if she had made a tragic mistake by running away from him on that traumatic afternoon. If she had stayed—if she had told him the truth—could they have faced the danger together? Would he have been in any more danger if he'd known the truth than he had been since she'd left?

It broke her heart to think that the sacrifices she'd made for him, the pain she'd caused them both, had been unnecessary. It had been so much less painful to tell herself that she'd had no other choice.

"Gabe, I—"

He placed a finger over her mouth. "Not now," he muttered. "We'll talk later."

"Yes," she said with a sigh, sliding her arms around his neck. "Later."

He thrust into her and she arched upward with a strangled cry of pleasure and discomfort. It had been a long time...and her experience prior to that had been limited to the three glorious weeks she'd spent as Gabe's wife. And then the pleasure took over, and the discomfort was forgotten. She and Gabe were together again, so tightly joined that it seemed that nothing could rip them apart. She couldn't ask for anything more at this moment.

As Gabe had warned her, he climaxed quickly. But he made sure that Page found her own satisfaction only moments later. Shuddering in mindless fulfillment, she sobbed his name, holding him as though she would never let him go again.

When they'd recovered enough to move, he tugged her into his arms and settled her a bit roughly against his shoulder.

"Sleep," he said, his voice gruff with emotion and exhaustion. "We'll talk tomorrow."

Knowing she was a coward to be so relieved by the delay, she only nodded and allowed herself to go limp against him. He reached out to turn off the lamp.

Judging from the sound of his breathing, Gabe went to sleep almost immediately. Page lay awake a few minutes longer, wondering about what had just happened, worrying about the future, dreading the daylight and the problems it would bring. Savoring the pleasure of lying beside him again.

It occurred to her that Gabe had never made love to her before without telling her he loved her. He hadn't said the words this time. Fingering the ring he'd insisted she wear on her left hand, she couldn't help but question the very mixed signals he'd been sending her since he'd found her.

What *did* Gabe feel for her now? Other than desire, of course. She couldn't begin to read him.

She only knew that her feelings for him hadn't faded during the time she'd been away from him. If anything, she had fallen even more desperately in love with the man who now held her—and her heart—captive.

GABE WOKE a couple of hours later. Page was still sleeping, her auburn hair tumbled around her face.

He tried to concentrate on that unfamiliar color, tried to remind himself that this wasn't the woman he'd married. But despite his best efforts to protect himself from being hurt by her again, his stubborn heart refused to accept that she was a stranger. She was his wife. The woman he had loved from the day he'd met her.

Despite everything that had happened, he knew he still loved her. And he always would.

He wondered bleakly what price he would pay this time for acknowledging that love. If he lost her again now, he believed it just might destroy him.

Watching her sleep, he warned himself that Page was still wary of letting him close to her, still too deeply afraid to fully trust him to help her solve her problems. So, for now, they had to concentrate on finding the man who'd been stalking her, making sure that he never posed a threat to her or to anyone she loved again.

Only then would they be able to concentrate on themselves. Only then could they talk about forgiving, forgetting, and somehow forging ahead.

9

PAGE WOKE ALONE in the bed. Disoriented for a moment, she blinked and tried to remember where she was, why she was lying nude beneath a rough white sheet, why her body felt sore and wonderful, all at the same time. She pushed a strand of hair out of her eyes with her left hand, and her attention was caught by the gleam of gold on her finger.

Swallowing hard, she lifted her head from the pillow, looking for Gabe. The bathroom door stood open, revealing an empty room. The door that led into the living room was closed. She wondered how long she'd been asleep.

Draping the sheet around her, she padded into the bathroom. Twenty minutes later, she felt somewhat prepared to face Gabe. She'd had a quick shower, brushed her teeth, and dressed in jeans and a long-sleeved red knit top. She combed her fingers through her hair and left it to dry naturally, and didn't bother with makeup. She didn't want Gabe to think she'd taken any special pains with her appearance today.

She'd left her watch on the nightstand. As she strapped it on, she looked at the thin gold chain Gabe had tossed beside it. She glanced at the ring on her hand, but left it in place, leaving the chain on the nightstand. Gabe apparently wanted her to wear the ring, at least for now. So—for now—she would wear it.

She was all too aware that their lovemaking, spectacular as it had been, had changed nothing. She would still leave him if she thought there was no other way to protect him. And he still resented her for leaving him before.

She found Gabe in the kitchen a few moments later. The scent of fresh-brewed coffee made her mouth water.

"I thought you might be hungry," he said, turning from the stove.

Self-conscious, she tucked a strand of hair behind her ear. "A bit," she said, her voice sounding odd even to her. "What do we have?"

"Not much," he admitted. "Whoever stocked the place just threw in some basics. Eggs, milk, butter, bread, meat, cheese."

"Who *does* this place belong to, anyway? Why are the windows boarded up, but the electricity on? Who brought in fresh food?"

Gabe shrugged. "I don't know. Blake arranged it all somehow. Only a few hours after I agreed that we should, um, detain you for questioning, he had this place lined up and ready."

"'Detain me for questioning'?" Page repeated, her tone wry. "That's an interesting way to define a kidnapping."

Gabe set a carton of eggs on the counter and closed

the refrigerator door. And then he turned to Page, his expression uncharacteristically hesitant.

"I'm sorry if you were frightened," he said quietly. "I didn't know what else to do to find out what was going on with you. Blake assured me he wouldn't hurt you. He didn't, did he?"

"No," she admitted, shrugging off the momentary discomfort caused by the prick of the needle in her arm. "He was quite considerate, on the whole. Very efficient—as though kidnapping women was something he did often. Where did you find that guy, anyway?"

"He was recommended by the investigator I'd hired prior to him. The last guy couldn't get anywhere on the case, and he could tell I was getting frustrated with him. He gave me Blake's name and number. Apparently, Blake is well known in the industry."

"What's Blake's last name?"

"I have no idea."

Page blinked in surprise. "You hired a guy without asking his last name?"

Looking a bit sheepish, Gabe cleared his throat. "He didn't seem to think it necessary. I could tell from the first that he was good. And he said if he didn't find you, he wouldn't charge me anything. That was becoming important, since I'd spent so much on the other guys already."

Page fought down a wave of guilt. She had no idea that Gabe would go to so much expense looking for her.

It occurred to her again that she had gravely misjudged her husband.

"Did you know he investigated *you?*" she asked, trying to redirect her thoughts.

Gabe's smile was crooked, revealing just a glimpse of that intriguing dimple in his left cheek. "I heard. That's when I knew I'd finally hired the right guy. He let nothing escape him."

"How did he find me in Des Moines?"

"I don't know. He doesn't believe in explanations—only in results."

Page shook her head. "He seems a little spooky."

Gabe chuckled. "That's one word to describe him, I guess. And yet—I sort of like him."

Page wrinkled her nose and sighed. "Unfortunately, I sort of do, too."

"I think he can help us, Page."

Us. The word made a funny little quiver go through her middle. She'd thought of herself as alone against the world for so long that she was still having a hard time adjusting to the knowledge that there was someone—two "someones," actually—on her side now.

"I thought Detective Pratt could help me," she said, forcing herself to hold on to the pessimism that had propelled her for so long. "Look what happened to him."

"Blake will be better prepared. He's more aware of what he's up against."

And if Blake did somehow manage to bring an end

to this? Then what? Did Gabe imagine that they could simply go back to where they'd left off?

Page didn't have the courage to ask. Or even to contemplate the future. She would concentrate, instead, on getting through another day, alone with Gabe.

"I'll scramble some eggs," she said abruptly, brushing past him without meeting his eyes. "Why don't you pour us some coffee?"

GABE WASN'T SURE how to read Page this morning. She'd made their breakfast, served it and eaten it with only a minimum of conversation. She seemed to be avoiding his eyes, and yet he sensed that she watched him closely when she thought he wasn't looking. Her hand wasn't quite steady when she lifted her coffee mug to her lips.

It felt very much like an awkward "morning after." Which was ridiculous, considering that this woman was his wife, Gabe thought grumpily, eyeing the gold ring he'd replaced on her left hand last night.

He was relieved she hadn't taken it off. He would have insisted that she put it back on again. The rings they wore were a physical reminder of the promises they'd once made, the unbreakable partnership they'd forged. And Gabe didn't intend for Page to forget those promises again.

He wanted very badly to take her into his arms right now, to remind her forcibly of the strong bonds between them—legal, physical and emotional bonds. Remembering the way she'd responded to him in bed, he suspected that she wouldn't resist him, or deny that the bonds were still there, still binding.

But he knew they couldn't fully concentrate on their feelings for each other as long as there was a chance that they were in danger from the lunatic who had driven them apart. And so, he forced himself to keep the distracting emotions suppressed—at least for now.

"I have to check in at the office," he said when the dishes had been cleaned and put away. "I left a couple of things hanging when I took off Friday afternoon."

"Your business is doing well?" she asked a bit too casually.

He couldn't keep a hint of pride out of his voice. "Very well," he said. "I've got four crews working now, and enough jobs lined up to keep them busy for some time. And there are five full-time employees working in the office."

He didn't add that the business could have grown even more had he not spent so much effort and so much money hunting for her. As it was, he'd spent long hours at work, often making his calls about Page from the office. Even if he'd wanted a normal social life, there wouldn't have been time between his commitment to his business and his obsession with finding Page.

He'd spent more than a few nights sleeping on the couch in his office. Sometimes because he'd just been too tired to drive home. Many times because he simply hadn't been able to face going home alone again.

"I'm happy for you," Page said, looking at him fully

for the first time all morning. "I know it was your dream to make your construction business successful."

"It was *our* dream for a while." He couldn't resist pointing that out.

She bit her lip. "Yes," she said after a moment. "It was."

They stood for a moment looking at each other, memories hovering in the air between them. An undercurrent of grief swirled around them. Regrets. Unspoken wishes.

Gabe broke the spell by turning abruptly and stalking into the living room where he'd left the cellular phone.

He made his calls quickly. Without giving details, he told his secretary that he would probably be out of the office for the rest of the week and that she was to call him on his cell phone only in case of emergency. He would be checking in several times a day, he added.

"Your mother called this morning, Gabe," the secretary, Angela, informed him. "She wanted to know where you are, in case she needs to reach you."

Gabe exhaled and pinched the skin above his nose.

He wasn't quite ready to tell his family that he'd found Page. Especially since he had no idea at this point whether she'd be with him when he returned.

"Tell her I'm going to be tied up for a few days but I'll give her a call when I can," he said inadequately.

His mother would give him hell when she found out what he'd been up to, of course, but he would deal with that when the time came. He could only handle one difficult woman at a time, he thought as Page wandered into the room.

He set the phone aside. "Blake should be checking in soon."

Page perched on the edge of a chair. "And what do we do in the meantime?"

"We wait."

She twisted her fingers in her lap. "Oh."

The photographs were still lying on the coffee table. Needing something to do, Gabe reached out to put them back in the manila envelope in which Page had kept them. The shot of him leaving a restaurant with the attractive brunette was on top of the stack.

He looked up and met Page's eyes.

Gabe cleared his throat. "This, er, this was taken last year. It was a dinner date my sister coerced me into. I'd been working pretty hard, not taking much time off, and Annie thought it would be good for me to get out. She had a friend who'd been through a recent divorce and she thought the two of us would, er, have something in common. I didn't enjoy the evening much. I didn't see her again."

Page nodded, her expression carefully blank. "That photo arrived when I was in Ft. Wayne, Indiana, along with another shot of my friend in Alabama. I moved the following day."

"You, um, must have wondered who I was with."

Page looked away. "I assumed you were getting on with your life."

The lack of emotion in her voice annoyed him, particularly now, after that spectacular predawn interlude. "And that didn't bother you?"

"I didn't expect you to become a monk, Gabe."

Her voice had become a bit strained, as if she were having some difficulty in staying so detached.

He shook his head. "I still can't believe you thought so little of me. That you had so little faith in our marriage."

"You don't understand," she said, sounding suddenly weary. Dejected. "Why can't you accept that I only wanted what was best for you?"

They kept coming back to this same point, Gabe mused, rubbing his jaw. She insisted she'd had no other choice but to leave, and he kept asking himself if she had loved him as much as he'd once believed. As much as he had loved her.

He couldn't imagine any force on earth that could have made him leave Page three weeks after their wedding.

Page released a deep, rather mournful sigh and turned her face away from him. "I'm tired," she said, her voice small. "I...didn't get much sleep."

It was the first reference she'd made to the night before. Gabe had been rather carefully avoiding mention of their lovemaking. Maybe, he thought, because he still wasn't sure what it had meant to her. And because it had meant too damned much to him.

"Why don't you take a nap?" he suggested. "I have some paperwork in a briefcase out in my truck that I can work on for a couple of hours."

She nodded. "I think I will. Let me know if Blake calls with any information, will you?"

"Of course." He watched her walk a bit too quickly to the bedroom. She looked as though she was making a welcome escape.

"Page?"

She glanced over her shoulder. "Yes?"

"You won't jump out the window again?"

Her chin lifted in annoyance. "Not unless it becomes necessary."

It wasn't the answer he wanted, but he nodded. "Then you can close the door so I won't disturb you by moving around in here."

"How kind of you to grant me permission," she muttered.

She closed the door. In fact, she slammed it.

Gabe winced and rubbed a hand over his face.

The day hadn't exactly gotten off to a great start. He could only hope it would get better—and not worse.

BLAKE CALLED an hour or so later. "I have some information that might be of interest to you," he said.

"Now why doesn't that surprise me?" Gabe shook his head in amazement at Blake's proficiency. "What have you got?"

"Professor Wingate's son isn't dead. He was shot three times, and came damned close to dying, but he survived. His name is Phillip. He's in his early twenties now."

"He's alive? But Page said—"

"She was mistaken. Apparently, there was a common misconception that he died. He was hospitalized for a long time and there were no relatives to report on his progress. By the time he was released, Wingate's murder-suicide was old news."

Gabe could feel his pulse rate quicken. Page's stalker had reason to hate her. He wanted her to be alone—as he was. He had been infuriated at her threat to kill herself, to "take the self-serving way out," as he'd called it.

The pieces all fit.

"Where is he?" he asked.

"I wish I knew," Blake replied, his tone a bit grim. "He reportedly left his hometown just over three years ago. No one who knew he was still alive seems to know what became of him."

Just over three years ago. Again, the coincidence was too strong to discount.

"What do you know about him?" Gabe asked, confident that Blake would have already started checking the guy out.

"A loner in high school. Not well liked by his peers. No close friends that I could discover. He didn't get along with his father, but he seemed unusually close to his mother. He had an affinity for computers, electronic gadgetry...and cameras," he added meaningfully.

"Damn." Gabe felt his stomach clench.

"I'm having his senior yearbook photo faxed to me. I should have it within the hour. And then I'm taking it to the garage where I had Page's car towed. Apparently someone was there very early this morning, asking about the car. Wanting to know who'd brought it in. I want to see if anyone there recognizes the face in the photograph."

Gabe frowned. "You think he's found us that quickly?"

"I think he's found her car," Blake corrected. "And I'm beginning to wonder if that's how he's kept up with her all along. Didn't you tell me it's the same car she was driving when she left Austin?"

"You think he's had some sort of tracking device on it?" It sounded like something out of a spy movie—but then, everything that had happened to Page was hard to believe. No wonder she'd doubted that the police would find her story credible: Had Gabe not seen her terror firsthand, he might still be doubting it himself.

"That's something I'll check out," Blake promised. He sounded a bit chagrined that he hadn't already thought of it. "He shouldn't be able to track you and Page there, but don't take any chances. Keep an eye peeled."

"You can bet on that. Good job, Blake."

"Remember, we don't even know Phillip Wingate is the guy we're after."

"No. But it sounds like a damned good lead."

"That's what I thought. How's Page holding up?"

"She's resting."

"Any aftereffects from the sedative I gave her yesterday? Nauseau, rash, headaches?" Blake sounded a bit worried.

"Not that she's mentioned. I think she's just exhausted from the stress she's been under for so long." Gabe saw no need to add that her rest had been interrupted during the night.

"Good. She's really something, Gabe. It took a lot of strength for her to get through the ordeal she described to us."

Not at all certain he liked the open admiration in Blake's voice when he spoke of Page, Gabe said, "I'm fully aware of what Page has been through."

"Are you?" Blake murmured. "Are you really?"

Gabe didn't know what to say.

"Tell her I said to hang in there," Blake said after a beat of silence. "With any luck, this will all be over soon. I'll be in touch."

He disconnected before Gabe could form a reply.

This will all be over soon.

Blake had sounded so confident. And given the P.I.'s track record so far, Gabe had to share Blake's confidence.

And then what?

Assuming this ended satisfactorily, with the stalker put away and Page freed from his threats, what would happen next? Could they really return to Austin and take up their lives as though nothing had happened between them?

They'd been married almost three years, and yet they were still newlyweds in a way, having lived together only three weeks before this nightmare separated them. Both of them had changed while they were apart.

Had their feelings changed, as well?

Could they ever get back what had been taken from them?

Remembering that he'd promised to tell her when Blake called, he walked quietly into the bedroom. Page was still sleeping, lying fully dressed on top of the sheets. She was curled on her side, one hand lying palm-up beside her face in a pose that made her look deceptively fragile.

She was pale, he thought, studying her closely. The faintest of purple smudges beneath her eyes testified to the strain she'd been under. Despite Blake's doubt, Gabe was fully aware that it had taken an amazing amount of strength for Page to do what she'd felt she had to do during her ordeal.

As much as he regretted her decision to handle the danger on her own, Gabe still loved her. His love had survived the pain, the anger, the grief and the anguish of the past two and a half years. He didn't fully understand it. Nor could he have explained it had he been asked. But he knew it with a certainty no amount of self-argument could shake.

His assurance of his own feelings made it all the more important for him to believe that she loved him as fully in return. And that, he thought glumly, was something he still couldn't take for granted.

"Page?" Emotion made his voice gruffer than he'd intended.

She opened her eyes, instantly awake and alert, instinctively braced to react. It disturbed him to think her experiences had left her so wary and anxious.

"What is it?" she asked huskily.

He sat beside her on the edge of the bed and touched her shoulder reassuringly. "Blake called," he said. "You said you wanted me to tell you if he had news."

He could feel her relax slightly beneath his palm. She cleared the remnants of sleep from her voice. "What did he find?"

Gabe quickly recapped his conversation with the competent P.I.

Page looked dazed when he finished. "Professor Wingate's son is alive," she murmured, as though to convince herself. "And you and Blake really believe he's the one who's been tormenting me all this time? Who murdered Jim Pratt?"

"Obviously, we can't know that for certain with what little information Blake's gathered so far. But you have to admit the clues point in Wingate's direction. He was left alone by his father's actions. He could blame you—unjustifiably, of course—for setting off the chain of events that led to the tragedy. He was a whiz with computers and electronics. No one has seen or heard from him in almost three years. No one, perhaps, except you."

She shivered. "Oh, Gabe. If it *is* Phillip Wingate..."

"What if it is?" he asked gently.

She turned her face away. "Then maybe he does have reason to hate me."

Gabe's fingers tightened convulsively on her shoulder. "That's crazy," he said sharply. "You did nothing wrong, Page. You weren't to blame for his father's insanity."

"I ruined his life. Instead of dealing with the situation myself, I turned him in, had him fired. And when his wife called to beg for my help, I hung up on her."

"You were not wrong to ask for help," Gabe argued. "You had a right to the university's protection from its own staff."

"I should have just left," she murmured, lost in her old regrets. "I could have transferred to another school. Another state."

"You think the right choice would have been to run away?" Gabe exerted pressure on her shoulder to roll her onto her back so that she had to look up at him.

"Why can't you realize that running isn't the answer, Page? Whatever his problems, Wingate had already gone over the edge when he started harassing you. There's no way to know that he wouldn't have killed his wife and himself regardless of whether you reported him or not. Running away wouldn't have changed anything then—just as running hasn't solved anything this time."

"You're still alive," she said, her face flushed in response to his criticism.

"James Pratt is dead," Gabe responded. "And his murderer, whether Phillip Wingate or someone we haven't identified, is still out there, a threat to anyone who comes near him."

Her flush receded to leave her skin deathly pale. "I know Jim's dead. If I hadn't asked for his help…"

Gabe cursed viciously beneath his breath, exasperated by his inability to make her see reason.

She was so convinced that everything was her fault. That she, alone, bore responsibility for every crime the crazy Wingates had committed. That she'd been fully justified in running away to protect Gabe.

"You are not alone in this, Page," he said between teeth clenched in frustration. "You haven't been since the day I put my ring on your finger. You are my wife. Whatever happens in the next few days, we'll face it together. The way we should have from the beginning."

"If anything happens to you—"

"Then it happens," he cut in. "But it will be because I chose to get involved, not because of anything you've done. Can you understand that?"

He knew it wasn't what she'd wanted to hear. She wanted him to promise her that nothing would happen to him. That there was something she could do to guarantee his safety.

He didn't give her that reassurance. Truth was, he couldn't. No one could predict how this situation would end. But he wanted her to know that he was an active participant, not a helpless victim. An ally, not an opponent. An equal partner, not another responsibility for her to assume.

That stubborn old-fashioned streak in him wanted

her to see him as her protector. Her champion. Her husband, damn it.

He wanted her to need him as much as he'd needed her these long, lonely months.

She lifted a hand to his cheek. Her fingers were cold against his skin, and he could feel the fine tremors that ran through them. Her blue eyes were huge in her pale face, the pupils dilated with emotion. "I don't want you to be hurt," she whispered.

He caught her hand and planted a kiss in the palm. "Then don't run away from me again," he muttered.

"Oh, Gabe—"

He swooped down to kiss her into silence. Her arms locked around his neck, holding him to her.

He stripped her clothing away with urgent hunger. Rather than complain at his lack of finesse, she cooperated fully, helping him rid them both of the layers of fabric that separated them.

Only when they were pressed skin to skin, heart to heart, desire to desire, did Gabe allow himself to slow down and savor.

He made love to her slowly this time. There was so much lost time to make up for.

Page shuddered in climax, sobbing his name, her arms and legs locked tightly around him. Gabe closed his eyes, buried his face in her throat and surrendered at last to his own shattering release.

I love you. I love you. The words echoed in his mind, but he swallowed them. They were all he held back as he emptied himself deep inside her.

LIMP AND DAMP, Page lay against the sheets, staring at the ceiling and listening to Gabe's movements in the bathroom. She felt slightly battered, somewhat bemused, and utterly baffled by Gabe's behavior. One moment he was growling at her, still resentful of her leaving him, the next he was making love to her with a tenderness that turned her inside out.

Yet he still hadn't told her he loved her.

Would she ever fully understand him? Could he ever completely understand her?

How could two people love each other as much as she and Gabe had and still not know what lay inside their deepest hearts?

She stroked a cool film of perspiration away from her breasts, her hand lingering at her tummy. They'd made love twice now, and hadn't used any form of birth control. There'd been a time when they'd talked excitedly about starting a family, raising children together. Now the thought of being responsible for someone else petrified her.

A baby was so vulnerable. So helpless. And Page felt so woefully inadequate when it came to keeping her loved ones safe.

Not that the burden would all be hers, she mused slowly. If there was one thing she was beginning to understand about Gabe, it was that he took his commitments very seriously. He would willingly give his life for his child—just as he was willing to risk it now for her.

She wasn't alone anymore. Gabe had been repeating

that for days, but she was only now beginning to believe it. The knowledge terrified her as much as it elated her.

She couldn't bear to think about how devastated she would be to suddenly find herself alone after being with Gabe again, even for this brief interlude.

A sudden, shrill buzz from the nightstand made her jump, her hand flying to her throat. Realizing that it was Gabe's cell phone, she glanced toward the closed bathroom door.

It was probably Blake calling, she thought, reaching for the phone. Maybe he had more news for them. She flipped the instrument open and spoke into it. "Hello?"

"I've taken care of your nosy investigator," an ominously familiar voice snarled in her ear. "As a matter of fact, I'm calling from his phone. You've really blown it this time, Page. Kiss your devoted husband goodbye. Before this day ends, he'll be a dead man."

10

"*NO-O-O!*"

The anguished cry from the other room nearly stopped Gabe's heart. Dressed only in white cotton briefs, he threw open the bathroom door and charged into the bedroom, tautly prepared for whatever awaited him.

Page sat nude in the center of the bed, the sheet pooled at her waist, Gabe's cellular telephone clutched in her hand. She looked as though someone had punched her in the stomach.

"What is it?" he asked her sharply. "Is that Blake?"

Looking incapable of speech, she shook her head. Her eyes were filled with tears, her lips trembling.

Gabe took the phone from her and held it to his ear, but whoever had called had disconnected. He tossed the instrument aside and set his hands on Page's shoulders.

"Page, what's wrong? What did Blake say to you?"

"It...it wasn't Blake," she managed to say, her voice reedy. "Blake...Blake's..."

"Blake's *what?*" Gabe demanded, resisting an urge to shake the words out of her.

"Dead."

Gabe recoiled from the stark syllable, raw denial coursing through him. "No."

She stared through him, lost in her own horror.

This time Gabe did shake her, gently, but firmly. "Page, talk to me," he said, his voice urgent. "Who called?"

"Him." The word was said with revulsion, letting Gabe know exactly who she meant.

"Wingate?"

"If he's the one who has been following me all this time." She spoke mechanically, her face blank with shock.

"He told you he'd killed Blake?"

She nodded, almost imperceptibly.

Gabe swallowed a wave of guilt. Of stabbing regret.

"We don't know it's true," he said, trying to reassure himself as well as Page.

She shuddered. "*I* know. He killed him."

Gabe swore and sank to the bed. "How the hell did he get this number?"

"He said he was calling from Blake's phone."

Automatic redial. Gabe groaned and rubbed his forehead. "We have to do something. We'll go to the police."

"They can't stop him."

"Damn it, Page, he's only human. He can be stopped."

"He said you're next."

Her whispered warning made him set his jaw. "He wants to frighten you. To make you run again."

She twisted her hands in the sheet. "Maybe, if we aren't together—"

"No," he cut in flatly. "You aren't going anywhere without me. It's too late for that now. He knows I'm on to him. He knows I'm not going to give up. One way or another, this has to end now."

The look she gave him made his throat tighten. "Gabe, please," she begged, tears spilling down her cheeks.

He reached out and pulled her roughly into his arms. This time the feel of bare flesh pressed to flesh was comforting rather than arousing. "I'm not leaving you, Page. We'll handle this together."

She clung to him, shivering. "Promise me you'll be careful. Promise you won't take any chances."

"I'll take care of myself," he promised, his tone gruff. "And of you," he added, holding her more tightly.

He heard her swallow. And then she drew a deep breath and pulled away from him.

"I'll get dressed," she said, and he could almost see her pulling her composure together. "We'll go to the police."

Nodding in approval, he reached for his own clothes.

They dressed in silence. Gabe mentally rehearsed his speech to the local police, knowing it would be difficult to convince anyone of their bizarre tale. If only he knew what had happened to Blake...

Blake. He pictured the blond man's lazy smile and

quiet competence, and his stomach clenched in re-
morse. He'd had no idea that hiring Blake to find
Gabe's runaway bride would lead to this. Gabe didn't
even know if Blake had a family, or anyone to grieve
for him.

Springfield being the nearest town to the cabin, they
agreed to go to the police department there. Gabe told
Page to bring the photographs and Detective Pratt's
business card, the only physical evidence she had to
back her story. They wouldn't prove anything, of
course, but there was something rather ominous about
those grainy, covertly taken snapshots. Gabe only
hoped the Springfield police would find them as disturbing as he did.

They were headed for the door when the cellular
phone rang.

Page and Gabe both froze for a moment, staring at
each other. Slipping an arm around Page's shoulders,
Gabe lifted the phone to his ear, reminding himself it
could be his secretary. "Hello?"

"Gabe? Are you and Page okay?"

Gabe thought for a moment that his knees might
buckle in relief. "Blake?" he croaked.

Page gasped and sagged against him.

"Yeah," Blake said. "I'm calling from a pay phone.
The bastard got my cell phone."

"We thought the bastard had gotten *you*."

"He did. But not as badly as he thinks."

"You're hurt?"

"Yeah. Can you come?"

"Of course." Gabe was already moving, towing Page with him as he asked for directions.

THE PAY PHONE was attached to the end of a dilapidated strip center that held a coin-operated laundry, a used comic book store, a shoe repair shop and two empty storefronts. Few customers were patronizing the businesses and the parking lot was nearly deserted. Gabe and Page found Blake sitting on the rutted asphalt beneath the phone box, his knees drawn up, his head resting on top of them.

He looked like hell.

"We've got to get you to a hospital," was the first thing Gabe said when he saw the other man's condition. Blake's face was gaunt with pain, and the front of his once spotless pale yellow shirt was spotted with the blood that dripped slowly from an angry-looking gash on his forehead.

No one else in the rundown neighborhood had apparently even bothered to ask if he needed help.

Blake shook his head, then groaned when the movement apparently set off a fresh wave of pain. "No hospital," he said, fending off Page's hands when she reached out to check his injuries. "Just get me away from here."

"What did he do to you?" Gabe asked, eyeing the ominous hollows beneath Blake's shock-glazed blue eyes in concern.

"He shot me. In the back, damn the coward."

Gabe hissed a curse and went down on one knee to

examine Blake's back. The bullet had torn across Blake's left shoulder, leaving a ragged wound and a great deal of blood. Blood that was still oozing from the injury.

"Damn it, Blake, you *are* going to the hospital," Gabe said, sharing a quick, worried look with Page.

"No. The bullet just grazed me. It hit a metal phone box I was standing by when I was shot. The cut on my head came from a piece of metal that broke loose when the bullet hit."

Gabe looked instinctively at the phone box above Blake, but Blake shook his head. "Another phone. I'll tell you about it on the way back to the cabin."

"Are you sure we should go back there?" Page asked.

"I don't know how he could have found out about the cabin," Blake answered, his head drooping wearily. "If he'd known we were there, he wouldn't have been hanging around the garage, waiting for one of us to show up for your car."

"And if he's watching us now? Waiting to follow us?" Page asked, darting nervous looks around the nearly deserted parking lot.

"He won't follow us," Gabe said grimly. He only wished he *could* get his hands on the son of a bitch. But first he would make sure Blake and Page were safe.

"I still think we should take him to a hospital," Page fretted, nodding toward Blake, who looked as though he could keel over at any moment.

"No hospital." Blake sounded prepared to fight with

his last breath on that count. "I hate hospitals. I'll be okay."

He sounded, Gabe thought, as though he'd been through similar situations before. Gabe was becoming more curious all the time about Blake's background.

Blake looked up at Gabe. "I could use a hand," he said.

Gabe positioned himself at Blake's injured left side, Page on Blake's right. Swaying between them, he somehow made his feet cooperate as they moved slowly toward Gabe's truck.

A couple of bored-looking teenagers, cigarettes dangling from their slack lips, watched idly from outside the used comic book store. Another stringy-haired young man shuffled haltingly toward the pair, his attention focused on the cigarettes rather than the injured man being half carried across the parking lot.

Wondering what kind of neighborhood they were in where bullet wounds roused so little interest, Gabe opened the passenger door of his truck and managed to stuff Blake carefully inside.

"I'll bleed on your upholstery," Blake warned with a sorry attempt at a smile. "Don't you have a towel or something to put behind me?"

"Screw the upholstery," Gabe said succinctly. "Page, help him with the seat belt."

She nodded and cooperated, positioning herself in the center of the seat between the men as Gabe climbed behind the wheel.

"Did you get a look at the guy who shot you?" Gabe asked as he started the engine. "Was it Wingate?"

"I didn't see him," Blake admitted reluctantly. "The guys at the garage said the photograph I showed them didn't look much like the man who'd been asking questions about Page's car, but that doesn't mean much. It's an old photo of a clean-cut kid. The guy who hung around the garage this morning had long hair, a scraggly beard and dark glasses."

"What happened, Blake?" Page asked.

Blake exhaled deeply. "I was stupid. I fell neatly into a trap he'd set for me."

"How?"

"Joe—the mechanic at the garage—said the guy had slipped him a twenty and asked him to call if anyone else showed up asking about the car. I pulled a few strings and managed to trace the number Joe had been given to a pay phone in the neighborhood we just left."

Gabe didn't even ask what "strings" Blake had pulled in a town he'd supposedly never even visited before. Page was right, he decided. Blake *was* spooky. And damned lucky.

"The phone," Blake continued, "was sitting outside a dump of a restaurant that's closed Mondays, so the place was deserted. I drove around a few times, then pulled into the lot when I didn't see anyone. Something was taped to the phone. I got out to see what it was. I thought I was being careful, but..." His voice trailed into a snort of self-disgust.

"What was taped to the phone?" Page wanted to know.

"Yellow paper, black ink. Two words—'big mistake.' I started to turn to run for my van, and that's when he shot me. The shrapnel to the head dazed me enough that I went down. I lay there, playing dead, waiting for him to finish me off or get close enough to give me a chance to take him on, but the bastard just got into my van and drove away. My own van, damn it."

"We'll call the police when we get to the cabin," Gabe said, his foot pressed heavily to the accelerator, one eye on the rearview mirror. "We'll report your van as stolen, give them the license number and description, tell them the thief tried to kill you. At least they'll be looking for him. We might have had trouble getting help with a stalker, but carjackers get attention these days."

Slumped against the back of the seat, his eyes closed, Blake murmured, "Good idea."

"Why didn't you call us from the phone where you were hit?" Page asked, sounding puzzled.

"He'd disconnected it. I had to walk half a mile to the one where you found me."

"Bleeding? And no one tried to help you?" Page sounded disgusted, but not entirely surprised. After hearing what she'd been through in the past couple of years, Gabe could understand her reaction.

"I didn't ask for help," Blake murmured.

Page set a hand on his arm. "I'm so sorry this happened to you, Blake. You were trying to help me. You didn't deserve to be hurt."

Blake shook his head. "Don't apologize. You aren't to blame. Wingate—or whoever pulled the trigger—is the only one at fault here, discounting my own stupidity for getting out of my van in the first place."

Gabe thought it would be a while before Blake stopped berating himself for that mistake. He was pleased, though, that Blake had unconsciously echoed Gabe's own assurances that Page could not hold herself accountable for anything this madman did.

Gabe made sure that no one followed them to the cabin.

They got Blake inside and deposited him facedown on the bed. More experienced than Gabe with first aid, Page sent him to report the stolen van and then prepare a meal while she cleaned and bandaged Blake's wounds.

She was fussing at Blake before Gabe left the room.

"The cut on your head probably needs stitches," she said. "You'll have a scar."

"Scars are devastatingly attractive to women," Blake quipped. "Macho and mysterious."

"Give me a break," Page muttered. "And be still," she added crossly, making Blake chuckle weakly even as he inhaled in protest at the sting of the antibiotic she applied to his shoulder.

Despite the circumstances, Gabe found himself reluctant to leave Page alone with Blake in the bedroom, good-naturedly squabbling like old friends.

Stupid, he told himself, shaking his head. This was definitely not the time to start acting like a jealous idiot. He was grateful beyond words that Blake wasn't badly injured...or worse. He really did like the guy.

And besides, Gabe and Page needed all the help they could get right now.

The police officer Gabe talked to seemed skeptical of the story, particularly when Gabe said that Blake—the victim—was presently unavailable to give a statement.

"He's injured," Gabe explained. "The carjacker tried to kill him."

"Then I'll send someone to the hospital where he's being treated," the officer offered.

"He doesn't like hospitals. My wife is taking care of him. After he's had a chance to eat and rest, we'll bring him in and tell you the rest of the story. In the meantime, you have the description and license number of the stolen van. Can't you put out a warrant on that basis?"

After some further hemming and hawing, the officer agreed to file the report. Gabe gave his number for the officer to call if the van were found.

He was grumbling beneath his breath when he disconnected the call and went into the kitchen to open a couple of cans of soup for dinner.

He was understanding better all the time why Page had been so reluctant to relate her bizarre tale to anyone. Were Gabe not squarely in the middle of it, he might have difficulty believing it himself.

"THERE. That should keep it clean."

"I'd say so," Blake responded to Page's comment, peering over his shoulder with a comical expression. "You've got enough tape on me to wrap a Buick."

"Well, excuse me. I don't have a great deal of experience bandaging gunshot wounds," she retorted, setting the nearly empty roll of adhesive tape back into the first-aid kit Gabe had unearthed from the bathroom. She'd been hesitant, at first, about working on Blake, but he'd teased her out of her self-consciousness and her fear of hurting him. She thought a bit wistfully that she and Blake were rapidly becoming friends. And, after the past two and a half years of being alone, she knew the value of friendship.

A look of regret on his face, Blake held his tattered, bloodstained yellow shirt on one finger. "The shirt's a goner," he muttered. "Damn. It was one of my favorites."

"I'm sure Gabe will lend you one."

"But I really liked this one. Cost me a fortune, too."

"Look at it this way, Blake. You've still got a pulse," she reminded him more matter-of-factly than she felt, playing along with his light tone.

He nodded. "There is that."

And then he smiled. "Thanks for patching me up, Page. You did a good job."

"You should have gone to the hospital."

"Don't start that again. Hospitals are terrible places. People die there."

"They're also saved there."

He grunted. "Not in my experience."

For a moment, a flash of bitterness in his eyes startled her. Blake had seemed the footloose, live-for-the-moment type to her, not a man to harbor deep emotions. Apparently she'd been wrong.

Before she could ask why he had such distrust of hospitals, he shoved himself to his feet. "Let's go find out if Gabe—"

He swayed. Page steadied him before he fell.

"You stood too fast," she scolded, eyeing his sudden pallor in concern. "You've lost more blood than you realize, Blake. You're going to have to take it easy for a while."

He allowed himself to lean against her for a moment. "Sorry," he murmured. "Guess I got a little cocky."

"Something tells me that's nothing new for you," she teased gently, supporting him with her shoulder.

Gabe found them that way, Blake's good arm around Page's shoulders, hers wrapped around his bare waist, their heads close together. Gabe's ferocious scowl made Page sigh. Just how far did his distrust of her extend?

"Dizzy spell," Blake explained quickly to Gabe, obviously seeing the same signs of masculine possessiveness Page had noticed. "Stood too fast."

Gabe stepped forward quickly to relieve Page of Blake's weight. "I'll help you into the kitchen," he said a bit brusquely. "You could probably use some food to build your strength. I warmed some soup."

Page stepped out of the way. "He could use a couple of painkillers, but he refused to take any," she said.

"They'd make me groggy. I need to stay alert," Blake explained, as he had the first time she'd offered the potent pills she carried in her purse for emergencies.

His precautions worried her as much this time as they had before. "You said he couldn't find us here."

She saw the look Gabe and Blake exchanged before Blake murmured, "I like to be prepared."

Shaking off Gabe's assistance, Blake lifted his chin and braced his feet, demonstrating that he could stand without support. Gabe gave him a clean blue chambray shirt to wear over the bandages. The shirt was a bit large on Blake, who had a slighter build than Gabe's muscular frame, but he buttoned it without comment. And without help. And then he managed to get to the kitchen on his own strength.

Vaguely annoyed at the entire male gender, Page followed.

"Let's assume that it is Phillip Wingate," Blake proposed a few minutes later, seated behind a steaming bowl of canned vegetable beef soup. "We know he's young and intelligent. And obviously insane."

"Where's he been living the past couple of years?" Gabe asked. "How's he been supporting himself?"

Blake shrugged. "I'd bet he's basically homeless. A drifter, trailing Page from place to place, begging or stealing to get by. Maybe even following her lead and taking odd jobs from time to time. That would fit the profile of an obsessed stalker. As for the photographs, he's either made a few side trips to snap them, or hired someone to take them for him. My money would be on him taking them himself. He's too much of a loner to work with a partner, even on a limited basis."

"He's consumed with thoughts of Page," Gabe muttered, staring into his bowl as though hoping to find a solution there. "Making her miserable has been his only goal these past thirty-odd months."

Blake nodded. "Which is why he didn't hurt her. Without her to torment, he basically has nothing to live for."

"Which means," Page interrupted, refusing to be left out of the discussion, "that I'm relatively safe. If I go away and make sure he believes that neither of you know where I am, he'll leave you both alone."

"Forget it." Gabe's voice was flat. His eyes bored into her, daring her to argue.

"It wouldn't help, Page." Blake agreed with Gabe. "Even if you were willing to spend the rest of your life running from him—and that's not something Gabe and I can accept—it wouldn't guarantee anyone's safety, including your own. The guy's crazy. He hates Gabe and he hates me, just because we're on your side."

Gratitude and fear warred equally inside her. "But—"

"It's not an option, Page," Gabe insisted. "You aren't leaving again, not if I have to handcuff you to my own wrist. Is that clear?"

"I make my own decisions," she snapped, irked by his uncompromising tone.

"Not when they're made on my behalf," he retorted, his jaw stubbornly set.

Their eyes locked. Held. Page could almost feel the sparks fly between them as stubborn willfulness clashed with inflexible determination.

"Soupspoons at twenty paces?" Blake asked whimsically, breaking the tension. "Loser has to eat the rest of this delightful swill."

Gabe cleared his throat and dipped unenthusiastically into his soup. Page bit her lower lip and turned her attention to the rest of her own unappetizing meal.

For a moment a taut silence reigned in the rustic cabin kitchen.

Again it was Blake who lightened the mood. "So," he said. "Since there's nothing else we can do about finding Wingate for the moment, why don't we get to know each other better. If you were a Pop-Tart, what flavor would you be?"

She was startled into a quick laugh. "That's a stupid question."

"Yeah, but you have to admit it's original," he quipped.

Blake was smiling, looking perfectly at ease, but Page saw the lines of pain still etched around his eyes and mouth, and the sallow cast beneath his lightly tanned skin. She knew what he was doing, and she was grateful that he wanted to take her mind off the danger for a little while. He must know how long it had been since she'd sat around a kitchen table and exchanged frivolous small talk. Maybe he even understood how much it meant to her to be able to do so now, if only for a few stolen moments.

Gabe's hand fell suddenly on her thigh beneath the table. He squeezed lightly, in what might have been an apology.

"I know what flavor she'd be," he said, obviously forcing a smile. "Strawberry. Page has a major passion for the taste and scent of strawberries."

Blake wiggled an eyebrow. "I'll keep that in mind."

Gabe turned a fierce, exaggerated scowl toward the other man. "No one is arousing my wife's passions except me," he growled, his hand still resting on her thigh.

Blake gulped loudly and held up his hand in surrender. "I hear ya', boss."

Page's smile felt strained. Even through the fabric of her jeans, she could feel the warmth of Gabe's hand, and she couldn't help but react.

She'd once accused Gabe of being rather primitive when it came to his views on marriage. She'd found his "me-Tarzan, you-Jane" tendencies both daunting and endearing, but he had promised her he would never treat her as anything but an equal partner in their marriage.

She was beginning to understand now that possessiveness and protectiveness were as much a part of her husband's nature as the passions that sometimes overwhelmed her.

He regarded himself as her protector, which was making it very difficult for him to accept that she'd viewed him as the one to be protected. She should have realized he would react that way. But didn't he understand that she had the same primal, instinctive need to defend the man she loved?

IT WAS GETTING DARK outside. Blake had put in a call to the Springfield police, who, after asking more questions, had admitted they had no leads on his van.

He was asked again to come to the station; he stalled by claiming he needed to rest and recover from his injuries. He promised to go in the next morning. The officer wasn't pleased, but Blake used his considerable charm to end the call on a conciliatory note.

"For all we know, the punk is watching the police station now," Blake explained to Page and Gabe after disconnecting the call. "That's what I would be doing in his shoes if I didn't know where else to look."

"We could set up a trap of some sort. Have the police waiting nearby," Gabe murmured, his forehead creased with thought.

Page knew Gabe felt unprepared to deal with this ugly situation. The skills he'd developed running his construction company hardly seemed applicable now. And yet, oddly enough, she felt confident that Gabe could handle whatever he encountered during the next hours.

She had finally learned not to underestimate the man she loved.

"That's an option," Blake acknowledged. "But since we don't know where Wingate is—or, for that matter, if it *is* Phillip Wingate who's after us—we have to be careful about how we approach the police."

"So what are we going to do?" Page asked, rubbing her hands over her forearms against a sudden chill in the cabin's tiny living room. "We can't hide here forever."

"We don't intend to," Gabe assured her. "Blake and I are going to make some plans."

"You aren't leaving me out," she protested.

"Of course not," he assured her quickly. A bit sheepishly. "You'll plan with us, of course."

"Nice recovery," Blake murmured with a slight smile.

Page glared at both of them.

Gabe shook his head and held up a hand. "Let's call a truce," he said. "We're in this as a team. We have to work together, not argue among ourselves. Agreed?"

After a moment Page sighed and said, "Agreed."

Gabe gave her a smile of approval. She had to look away to keep him from seeing her very feminine reaction to that quick flash of teeth and dimple.

Blake propped his feet on the coffee table and leaned his head against the back of the couch. Page could tell he'd used nearly all his reserves of stamina. He needed rest. He rubbed his head, as if it throbbed. Looking at the nasty bruise beneath the bandage she'd applied, Page was sure that he had a pounding headache.

"Blake, won't you at least take an aspirin?" she

asked. "I have some in my purse. The pain pills would help you more, but an aspirin will give you some relief without making you groggy."

He gave her a faint smile. "Thanks, but I'm allergic to aspirin. I'll be okay."

"I have acetaminophen capsules in the glove compartment of my truck," Gabe volunteered, looking at Blake in a way that told Page he shared her concern.

"I'll get them," Page volunteered, jumping to her feet, eager to help. "Gabe, why don't you pour him a glass of water?"

She realized that both men had tensed as she moved toward the door, their expressions doubtful. It took her only a heartbeat to figure out why they'd gone so still.

She scowled, and faced them both with her fists on her hips. "I'm not going anywhere except to the truck for the pills," she snapped. "I wasn't planning an escape."

Gabe seemed to relax. "Sorry," he muttered. "But with your track record so far..."

"Better shut up while you're ahead, Gabe," Blake advised with characteristic humor.

Looking straight at Gabe, Page held her chin up proudly and said, "I'm trusting you to help me, Gabe. Now you have to trust me."

Gabe grimaced and reached into the front pocket of his jeans. "You'll need these," he said, holding up the keys to his truck.

He tossed them to her. She caught them deftly in her right hand. She allowed her lips to curve into a slight smile of gratitude before she turned and walked outside without another word, feeling as though they'd just taken a very big step in their complex relationship.

There were no lights outside the secluded little fishing cabin. Long shadows fell across the small, cleared lot. The newly risen moon provided barely enough illumination to lead Page from the tiny front porch to Gabe's truck, which was parked in the gravel driveway.

The night was cool, with a hint of rain in the breeze that came off the lake. Page shivered and hurried to the truck, anxious to be safely back inside with Gabe and Blake.

She had just put the key into the door lock when something cold and hard pressed against her temple.

"You people are really stupid," a voice she'd heard in too many nightmares murmured from close behind her. "Sometimes I wonder why I've wasted so much time with you."

She opened her mouth instinctively to scream. He slapped a grimy hand over the lower half of her face.

"Scream and I take down the first man who comes out the door," he warned. His strong arms pinned her to him, and the gun in his right hand gleamed softly in the pale moonlight.

Her heart seemed to stop. "No. Please," she begged, her voice muffled by his hand. "Don't hurt them."

He pushed her toward the truck. "Get in. We're going for a ride. You're driving."

She resisted for a moment, but his fingers bit into her

arm. "You've got a choice, Page," he snarled, motioning with the gun. "Get in the truck or I shoot you on the spot. And then I'm going after them."

Her eyes flooding with tears, she surrendered. She had no doubt that he would do just as he threatened. And she simply couldn't allow it.

She slid into the open door of the truck.

I'm sorry, Gabe. Please forgive me. And stay safe.

11

GABE FILLED a plastic tumbler with cold water from the tap, berating himself for letting Page see his momentary doubt when she'd offered to go out for the pills. He'd been the one who'd insisted they had to start acting as a team. He couldn't blame her for being annoyed with him for behaving as though he were afraid to let her out of his sight.

She trusted him. He found that knowledge encouraging. Maybe by the time this was over, he could become as convinced that she loved him.

He turned the water off just as Blake yelled from the other room. *"Gabe!"*

Gabe dropped the tumbler and ran. Blake was standing in the open doorway of the cabin, glaring outside with an expression of shock and fury.

Gabe skidded to a halt, staring in disbelief at the taillights of his truck as they disappeared down the gravel road and became obscured by trees. "She didn't—"

Blake slammed his fist against the open door. "She took off. Damn it, she's gotten away from us again!"

Gabe shook his head, remembering the expression on Page's face when she'd promised not to run. She'd looked so hurt at their doubt, so sincere in her reassurances. "I can't believe she ran out on us."

"Believe it," Blake said irritably. "I heard the truck start, and by the time I got to the door, she was already halfway down the driveway. I would have bet anything that we'd convinced her not to do this. We were stupid to trust her."

Something was wrong. Gabe felt it all the way to his toes. And he couldn't believe that Page had decided to try again to handle her problems on her own. Not after she'd looked at him the way she had and promised he could trust her. "We've got to go after her."

"In what?" Blake snapped. "She's got the truck. Wingate's got my van. We're stranded here."

That ominous feeling was growing stronger by the moment. "Then we have to call someone. The cops. Anyone. Damn it, we have to stop her."

As though he suddenly shared Gabe's cold premonition, Blake calmed down and looked at Gabe with a frown. "What are you thinking?"

"She hasn't run again, Blake. She wouldn't leave us stranded here without a clue as to where she's gone."

"It certainly looks that way," Blake said slowly.

Gabe nodded tightly. "I know what it looks like. But it's not true."

He simply wouldn't accept it.

"So—what? You think she's headed for the nearest grocery? The closest pharmacy?"

"Not without telling us." Gabe was already reaching for his cellular phone.

"We have to find her," he muttered, more to himself than to Blake, snatching the instrument off the coffee table where he'd left it. "She needs—"

The phone rang in his hand.

Looking at Blake, Gabe held it to his ear. "Hello?"

"Do *not* call the cops. Not if you want to see her alive again."

The curt command was given in a voice that was unfamiliar to Gabe. But he would bet Page knew it all too well.

"Where is she? What have you done with her?" he demanded, his grip white-knuckled on the phone.

"You want her? Come and get her," the voice taunted.

Gabe had gone cold, right through to his bones. "If you lay a hand on her, I'll kill you, you bastard."

"You are persistent, aren't you? Haven't you figured out yet that she isn't worth your loyalty? All the time and money you've spent looking for her since she ran out on you—what a fool you are," the voice marveled. "She's a home-wrecking, two-bit tramp and you're just another besotted idiot who's fallen under her spell. What do you all see in her?"

The man sounded genuinely perplexed when he added, "How many more stupid men are going to have to die for her before I do the world a favor and get rid of her, hmm?"

"Don't hurt her." Gabe wasn't quite begging—but he knew he would, if he thought it would make a difference.

"You just don't understand, do you, man? *She* doesn't get hurt. It's the people who get near her who suffer. Are you still willing to take that risk? Or do you want to forget about her right now and go back to Texas? That's what I would do if I were you. I'd consider myself well rid of her."

Terror sharpened Gabe's tone. "I want her back. And I'm not going to rest until I have her. And if you hurt her, I won't rest until I've gotten to *you*. Is that clear?"

His threat was met with a gruff chuckle. "Okay, fine. If that's your decision, then come after her. I'll even tell you where she'll be. Oh, and bring your detective friend along," he added, all humor leaving his voice. "That's an order, not a suggestion."

Gabe shot a look at Blake, who hovered nearby, waiting impatiently to find out what was going on.

"You'll find your buddy's van a couple of hundred yards down the road from the cabin," the caller said. "The keys are in it."

He gave a few quick, curt directions to the rendezvous point, then warned, "And if you're thinking of doing something really clever, like bringing the cops with you, don't. They'd probably take me out, but not before I put a bullet in the bitch's head. To be quite honest, I don't care whether I survive this or not. You want to take the same chance with your wife?"

"I won't bring the police," Gabe said woodenly.

"Wise choice. You've got an hour, Conroy. If you take any longer than that, I'll assume you got smart and wrote her off. And then I'll make sure she never troubles you—or any other man—again."

"Wait, I—"

But the caller had already disconnected.

Gabe lowered the phone and looked bleakly at Blake. "He's got her."

Blake was watching him intently, visibly poised for action. "What did he say?"

Gabe briefly summed up the call, including the directions of where they could supposedly find Page. "He gave us an hour. We'll have to go in alone. If he sees any sign of police, he'll kill her."

"For all we know, he's already killed her," Blake said quietly.

Gabe's jaw tightened. "No," he said. "He wants her to witness whatever he plans to do to me."

He could only hope his words were true. He refused to believe that there was nothing he could do to save Page.

"You know it's a trap, Gabe. He has no intention of handing her over to you."

"I know. But I have to go. You, of course, have no obligation to go with me."

Blake ran a hand through his hair, wincing when his fingers brushed the bandage on his bruised forehead. He then took a deep breath, shifted his wounded shoulder beneath his borrowed shirt and said, "Come on, Conroy. Let's go get your wife."

"WHAT ARE YOU going to do with me?" Page studied Phillip Wingate as she asked the question, trying to understand his bizarre behavior.

He was pacing the length of the dirty, badly abused motor home he'd brought her to, muttering beneath his breath, scratching at his straggly hair and beard. He seemed to be carrying on a muttered conversation with someone she couldn't see, though she knew he was fully aware of her every movement as she huddled on a filthy built-in couch, watching him.

He looked at her with a scowl. "Shut up. I'm not in the mood for conversation."

He should have been a nice-looking young man. In his early twenties, he was sandy-haired and blue-eyed—as his father had been, Page remembered. But Phillip's eyes glittered with a feverish intensity that didn't require a psychiatric degree to diagnose.

He'd allowed his hair to grow long and shaggy, and it needed washing. His rather pathetic attempt at a beard was patchy and tangled. It didn't hide the thick scar that marred one side of his face.

He walked with a limp. His shuffling gait made Page remember where she'd recently seen him—in the parking lot of the rundown shopping center where she and Gabe had found Blake.

Two teenagers had been smoking outside the comic book store, she remembered. A third young man had approached them as if to bum a cigarette, just as Page and Gabe had helped Blake to his feet and across the parking lot. It had been Phillip Wingate. And he'd approached the smoking pair from the direction of

Gabe's pickup.

Page and Gabe had been too concerned with Blake's injuries to watch Gabe's truck. Wingate had been keeping Blake under surveillance, knowing he would call for help. And when they'd arrived, he'd attached some sort of transmitter to Gabe's truck, allowing him to locate the cabin. He'd told her that on the way here, after he'd made the call to Gabe. Wingate had seemed quite proud of his skills—in fact, he'd called himself "a genius."

Eyeing the complicated-looking electronic equipment that took up most of the otherwise-impoverished interior of the motor home, Page mused that Phillip Wingate probably did have a genius-level IQ—as his father had. She couldn't help but be saddened that Wingate, Senior, had also passed down his emotional instability.

"I didn't ask Gabe to find me," she tried to explain again. "He searched for me on his own. I begged him to go away and leave me alone, but he wouldn't. If you let me go now, I'll disappear again. I'll hide so well that he'll never find me. That's what you want, isn't it? For me to be alone?"

"You've already been there," Wingate snapped, patting the gun he'd stuck into the waistband of his dirty jeans. "Now I think it's time for you to find out how it feels to watch someone you love die."

Her stomach clenched in fear. "I won't let you hurt him," she whispered. "You'll have to kill me first."

"You know, Page, I really don't care," Wingate said with a shrug. "You first, or him. Either way, you're both dead. Your friend, as well. It comes full circle tonight, doesn't it? A husband, a wife, and an innocent bystander. All shot because of you."

He was insane. And he was fully prepared to kill—and to die.

There would be no reasoning with him, Page thought sickly. Nothing she could say would change his mind now. He was trapped in the horror of his own past, intent on reliving the nightmare of his parents' deaths. And he planned to end it tonight.

She'd heard the call Wingate had made to Gabe, using the cellular phone he'd stolen from Blake. And she knew Gabe would come for her, regardless of the danger.

She drew more tightly into herself, desperately searching her mind for a plan. She would do whatever it took to guarantee Gabe's safety—even if it meant sacrificing her own.

WINGATE HAD THE GUN in his hand when he opened the side door to the motor home in response to Gabe's knock. He looked from Gabe to Blake, who stood close by.

"You made good time," he commented. "Fifteen minutes to spare. Come in. Oh, and I suppose I should add the usual warning for you both to keep your hands where I can see them, and to make no sudden moves."

Gabe spotted Page the moment he stepped into the

rank-smelling camper. She was sitting on a tattered couch, her hands in her lap, her eyes huge and apologetic. "I'm sorry," she mouthed.

He nodded and, satisfied that she was unharmed, turned his attention back to Wingate.

The young man was gazing from Gabe to Page with a strange smile crooking his mouth. Gabe wondered who Wingate was seeing when he looked at them. His parents? Gabe had never been this close to insanity before, and the expression in Wingate's eyes chilled him.

Gabe felt a ripple of panic deep inside him, but he ignored it. One way or another, this had to end now.

Wingate had backed against a cluttered counter in the confined space, the gun uncomfortably steady in his hand as he faced Gabe, Blake and Page. Page stood slowly, her hands outstretched, and moved closer to Gabe. Wingate watched her, but didn't protest. He was still wearing that peculiar smile with which he'd greeted Gabe and Blake.

Gabe broke the eerie silence. "What now?" he asked.

"I've been waiting for this for four years," Wingate replied. "Forgive me if I take a moment to savor it."

"Let Gabe and Blake go," Page said, sounding desperate but not very optimistic. "They aren't a part of this. They've done nothing to you."

"Innocent bystanders," Wingate murmured. "Just as my mother was. As I was. We'd done nothing, either. But she's dead. And I'm alone. You know how it feels to be alone, don't you, Page? It's hell."

"I'm sorry about your family, Phillip," Page whispered. "But there was nothing I could have done to prevent it. I wasn't even in Alabama when it happened. I'd already moved to Texas."

"You made my father fall in love with you," Wingate snarled. "You made him obsessed with you. He couldn't forget you, even after you destroyed him and then left town. My mother tried to make him forget you, but he wouldn't. He killed her because she wasn't you."

Gabe felt Page shudder. He reached out to take her icy hand in his own, never taking his eyes from Wingate.

"You blame Page for destroying your father," Blake said, as still and watchful as Gabe. "Yet you've let her do the same to you. You're as obsessed with her as he was. Why don't you forget her? Get on with your life. Nothing you do now can change the past."

The expression on Wingate's face made Gabe's blood run cold.

"Life?" Wingate murmured. "I don't have a life. My father killed me the day he shot my mother. That's why there's nothing any of you can do to stop me now. Unlike the rest of you, I don't really care if I'm still breathing by morning. But I can guarantee you that I'll take at least one of you with me."

Wingate pointed the gun at Page, though Gabe knew he was watching all of them for the least sign of movement. Any provocation would set him off.

"What's it going to be, Page?" Wingate asked. "You were only thinking of yourself when you destroyed my father. You left him to die. Here's your chance to do the same with this poor fool. Show him how stupid he's been to love you all this time."

From the corner of his eye, Gabe watched as Page frowned and shook her head. "I don't understand what you mean," she said.

"I'm telling you to go," Wingate explained lightly. "Run. Save yourself. You can leave, right now, and I won't do a thing to detain you. I'll kill these two, of course, but what do you care about that? There will be other men who'll fall under your strange spell. Assuming, of course, that I'm not there to stop them."

"You'll let her leave?" Gabe asked skeptically. "Just like that?"

Wingate nodded. "She can go. Or she can stay and die with you."

Gabe exchanged a quick, questioning look with Blake, who looked as baffled as Gabe felt.

Wingate jerked his chin toward the door. "Last chance, Page. Take off. Run. You're so very good at that."

"Go, Page," Gabe urged, hoping that Wingate would keep his word. "Blake and I can take care of ourselves."

Page didn't move. "I'm not leaving."

"Gabe's right, Page," Blake murmured. "We'll be all right. He's giving you a chance to get out. Take it."

"I'm not leaving," Page answered fiercely.

She glared at Wingate, her eyes narrowed, her face pale but determined. "Do you really think I've spent all this time running to save *myself?*" she demanded angrily. "You can shoot me now, if you want. But I won't let you hurt Gabe."

Wingate's laugh was short, incredulous. "You won't *let* me? How do you plan to stop me?"

"Any way I can," she challenged.

Gabe swallowed a groan. He sensed that Blake had gone tense. Ready. "Page—"

"I love you, Gabe. I always have, more than my own life. And I'm not leaving you now."

He accepted her flat refusal with mixed emotions. High among them was an unexpected serenity that came from knowing, at last, that she really did love him. Now—and the day she had left him.

He knew, now, exactly how it felt to be willing to sacrifice his own life for the one he loved...just as Page had for him two and a half years ago.

He moved to stand in front of her, his eyes on Wingate, fully prepared to use his own body to shield her. "Let's talk about this," he suggested, feeling the tension mounting in the air.

"I'm tired of talking," Wingate snapped. "Tired of hurting. Tired of all of it. It's time for it to end."

He raised the gun.

Even though he'd been warned what to expect, Gabe was startled when a knife suddenly sliced through the air, slamming into Wingate's right shoulder.

Wingate staggered. The gun wavered.

Both Gabe and Blake threw themselves forward.

Gabe heard Page scream when the gun went off, so

close to him it nearly deafened him. And then he had Wingate beneath him, fists and feet flailing, the air filled with shouts and curses.

The doors to the motor home crashed open. More bodies poured into the already cramped space. Electronic equipment shattered.

Something hit Gabe in the back of the head, hard. He attributed that hit to the weakness that was suddenly overtaking him.

Someone pulled him off Wingate. Gabe hadn't realized he'd wrapped his hands around Wingate's throat until a beefy police officer pried them away.

"We've got him," the officer said. "Move over there, out of the way. We'll—hey, you're bleeding pretty bad."

"Gabe?" Page was at his side, kneeling next to him on the filthy carpeted floor. He wasn't sure how he'd gotten onto his back, but he seemed incapable of rising.

"Oh, my God," she gasped, placing a hand on his chest. "Oh, Gabe, no."

Blake looked over Page's shoulder. He hissed a curse from between his teeth and started unbuttoning his borrowed shirt.

"Here," he said, shrugging it off and bundling it into Page's hands. "Keep this pressed to the wound. I'll make sure an ambulance is on the way."

Wound? Gabe wondered where, exactly, he was hurt. He seemed to be numb below the neck, though he sensed that pain hovered just out of reach. And that, when it hit him, it was going to be major.

There was a great deal of activity going on around him. A lot of noise and confusion. The motor home was too small for all the commotion. It rocked dizzyingly as people bustled in and out.

Gabe reminded himself to congratulate the police on getting there so quickly, handling everything so efficiently. He knew he and Blake hadn't given them much to go on with the hasty call for help they'd made on the way here.

He'd have to compliment Blake, too. That knife trick had been truly amazing.

"Gabe, talk to me. Can you hear me?" Page sounded as though she'd been speaking to him for a while.

He tried to concentrate on her face, which hovered so close to his own. She was pressing hard against his chest with both hands, tears running unchecked down her cheeks. He frowned.

"Don't cry," he said, finding it surprisingly difficult to form the words. "I'm okay."

"He shot you." Her breath caught. "Oh, Gabe."

He lifted a hand to her face. It felt as though his arm weighed a ton.

"I'll be all right," he promised.

He hoped he told the truth. The feeling was returning to him now. He could almost imagine that Blake's knife had sliced into *him* rather than Wingate, and that the wound had been filled with burning embers. Something told him he was just beginning to experience the full extent of the pain yet to come.

He glanced downward, then wished he hadn't. The

shirt Page held pressed to the right side of chest was rapidly becoming soaked with blood.

"Looks like I'll have a scar," he murmured, trying to ease the agony reflected in her eyes. "Blake says they're devastatingly attractive to women."

Page tried to smile. "You're devastating enough already."

And then her weak attempt at a smile faded into a sob. "I'm so sorry," she whispered. "I tried so hard to prevent this."

"I know," he murmured. "That was why you left me. I understand that now."

"I wanted you to be safe," she whispered, her words barely audible above the turmoil around them. "I couldn't bear to have anything happen to you because of me. And now it has, despite my efforts."

"I'll be...okay," he murmured, but his voice was fading, his vision blurring. The pain was beginning to overwhelm him. He focused intently on Page's face, unwilling to let her out of his sight again.

Now that he finally had her back, he didn't want to think about how close he'd come to losing her.

Page pressed harder on his chest. "Gabe, please. Hold on," she pleaded, her voice thick with tears. "I love you so much."

"Love you," he managed to whisper. "I...never stopped."

He closed his eyes.

"*Gabe!*"

"Okay, ma'am, move aside. We'll take over from here." The voice was a strange one, deep and brusque.

Gabe felt hands on him, people around him. "Page?" he asked without opening his eyes.

"I'm here, Gabe," she assured him, her voice sounding further than before, but still close.

"Don't leave me."

"I won't," she promised. "I'll never leave you again."

Satisfied with her answer, he let the pain engulf him.

BLAKE SLIPPED an arm around Page's shoulders and pulled her out of the way of the medics and police officers swarming through the motor home. He seemed oblivious to the chaos, and to the evening chill that permeated the metal walls, wafting across his bare chest.

"We should go outside," he murmured. "Give them room to work."

Her eyes were locked on Gabe's bloodless face. "I promised I wouldn't leave him."

"We'll only step outside," he assured her. "You'll probably be allowed to ride with him in the ambulance, once they get him ready to transport."

She looked at him through tear-glazed eyes. He was battered and bruised and still obviously in pain, but his only concern now seemed to be for her. "You saw him, Blake. Do you think he'll be all right?"

She didn't like the doubt that flashed through his shadowed blue eyes before he forced a smile and nodded. "Sure he will."

Her breath caught in a sob. "If he'd only stayed in Austin, this never would have happened. He would have been safe."

"I saw him in Austin," Blake reminded her gently. "He was the most miserable guy I'd ever met. Nothing on earth could have kept him from finding you, Page. And I refuse to believe he went through all that only to leave you now. He'll pull through."

Page watched as Gabe was lifted carefully onto a narrow stretcher. She allowed Blake to lead her outside, out of the way of the paramedics and the police officers who hovered nearby, practically bristling with questions that Blake refused to answer until later.

Wingate had been taken away to have his own injuries tended. Page neither knew, nor cared, what would become of him.

Her only thoughts now were for Gabe…just as they had been for the two and a half years she'd spent away from him.

_____Epilogue_____

GABE DROVE his pickup into the double garage of his three-bedroom home, nodding in satisfaction when he saw the new maroon minivan parked in its usual space. After all this time, he still occasionally felt a mixture of pleasure and relief when he came home to find it there.

He climbed out of the truck, then reached in for the long white box that had been lying on the seat beside him. A faint scent of roses tickled his nose when he tucked the box under his arm. He'd bought a dozen long-stemmed blooms in strawberry red.

It was his fifth wedding anniversary, though he and his wife had actually lived together only a little more than two years, all told. And, while they'd had their share of problems to work out—as all married couples did—Gabe still considered himself a very lucky man.

He was greeted just inside the door by a gray cat, which meowed a welcome and wrapped itself around Gabe's ankles.

"Hello, B.J.," Gabe murmured, reaching down to tickle the cat's ears. He'd brought the kitten home to Page a few weeks after they'd returned from their ordeal in Springfield. She'd immediately burst into tears, which had worried him until she'd explained that the tears were in response to the thoughtfulness of his gesture. She'd named the cat "Buddy Junior"—B.J., for short.

"Where's Page?" he asked the affectionate cat.

As if in answer, B.J. yawned, turned, and walked lazily toward the den. With a chuckle, Gabe followed.

He found Page sitting cross-legged on the carpeted floor. She looked up to greet him with a radiant smile.

He smiled back, pleased to note that the shadows were all gone from her sky-blue eyes now.

She'd had nightmares for a while. They'd disappeared when she had finally convinced herself that Gabe would always be there to comfort her when she woke.

He bent to press a lingering kiss on her soft lips, immersing himself in the familiar taste and scent of her.

"Happy anniversary," he murmured when he reluctantly pulled back for air.

He handed her the box of roses. He could hardly wait for Page to open the gift he was saving until after dinner. He'd purchased airline tickets to Hawaii, and had booked a suite in a five-star hotel in Maui.

He'd been saving for a long time to finally give Page a real honeymoon.

"Oh, Gabe, thank you," she murmured, opening the box of roses with beaming pleasure. "They're beautiful. I love you."

"I love you, too," Gabe said easily.

And then he turned his attention to the six-month-old baby who lay on his back in front of Page, and was making an eager grab for B.J.'s temptingly close tail. Gabe reached out to lift his son into his arms. Stephen Blake Conroy squealed in slobbery delight when Gabe tickled his chubby tummy.

Gabe didn't mind in the least that their son would be going along with them on their honeymoon—and he knew Page would feel the same way.

Gabe's sister had volunteered to baby-sit, but Gabe had politely declined. He liked having his family close by, he'd explained a bit sheepishly. Maybe someday he and Page would take a few days off to themselves, but for now Gabe was perfectly content to be part of a happy threesome. Four, counting the cat.

Gabe brushed a kiss against his son's impossibly soft cheek. And then he wrapped an arm around his wife's shoulders and pulled her snugly against him. Life was good, he thought contentedly.

He and Page had been given a second chance at having it all, and they would spend the rest of their lives celebrating. Together.

HARLEQUIN®

Temptation®

COMING NEXT MONTH

#637 BRIDE OVERBOARD Heather MacAllister
Brides on the Run, Book II

Blair Thomason was going to take the plunge—into marriage, that is. But when she found herself on a yacht, about to marry a crook, she did the only thing she could—she jumped. Lucky for Blair, gorgeous Drake O'Keefe was there to pull her out of the Gulf. Except she'd barely escaped marrying one man, only to be stranded with another!

#638 ROARKE: THE ADVENTURER JoAnn Ross
New Orleans Knights, Book I

For journalist Roarke O'Malley rescuing a beautiful, sexy woman was second nature. But he knew better than to fall in love, especially with a woman who couldn't remember her past. Still, he couldn't abandon Daria Shea to the men who were determined to harm her. Too late he realized the greatest danger was losing his heart....

#639 RESTLESS NIGHTS Tiffany White
Blaze

Victoria Stone's erotic daydreams about a sexy gunslinger were harmless enough, until Zack DeLuca came along. Not even in her wildest imaginings had Victoria pictured herself responding so brazenly to a perfect stranger. And it was completely crazy to let him take her to a ghost town where all her fantasies were far too real....

#640 THE RETURN OF DANIEL'S FATHER Janice Kaiser
Ethan Mills was back and determined to claim his only son, little Daniel. One woman—and the wrath of a town—stood in his way. But Kate Rawley was soon defenseless in the face of Ethan's unyielding love for his child...and his overwhelming sexuality.

AVAILABLE NOW:

#633 THE GETAWAY BRIDE
Gina Wilkins

#634 WISHES
Rita Clay Estrada

#635 THE BLACK SHEEP
Carolyn Andrews

#636 RESCUING CHRISTINE
Alyssa Dean

Take 4 bestselling love stories FREE

Plus get a FREE surprise gift!

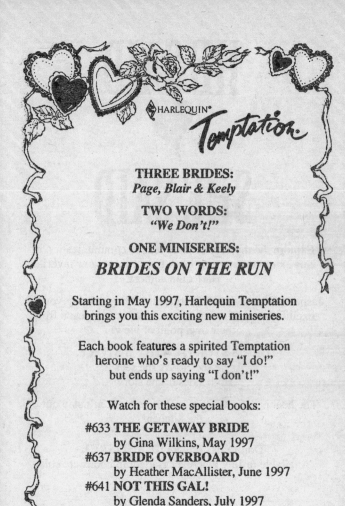

HARLEQUIN® *Temptation*

THREE BRIDES:
Page, Blair & Keely

TWO WORDS:
"We Don't!"

ONE MINISERIES:
BRIDES ON THE RUN

Starting in May 1997, Harlequin Temptation
brings you this exciting new miniseries.

Each book features a spirited Temptation
heroine who's ready to say "I do!"
but ends up saying "I don't!"

Watch for these special books:

#633 THE GETAWAY BRIDE
by Gina Wilkins, May 1997
#637 BRIDE OVERBOARD
by Heather MacAllister, June 1997
#641 NOT THIS GAL!
by Glenda Sanders, July 1997

Available wherever Harlequin books are sold.

HE SAID

♥

SHE SAID

Explore the mystery of male/female communication in this extraordinary new book from two of your favorite Harlequin authors.

Jasmine Cresswell and Margaret St. George bring you the exciting story of two romantic adversaries—each from their own point of view!

DEV'S STORY. CATHY'S STORY.
As he sees it. As she sees it.
Both sides of the story!

The heat is definitely on, and these two can't stay out of the kitchen!

Don't miss **HE SAID, SHE SAID.**
Available in July wherever Harlequin books are sold.

On the plus side, you've raised a
wonderful, strong-willed daughter.
On the minus side, she's using that
determination to find

A Match For
MOM

Three very different stories of mothers,
daughters and heroes...from three of your
all-time favorite authors:

GUILTY
by Anne Mather

A MAN FOR MOM
by Linda Randall Wisdom

THE FIX-IT MAN
by Vicki Lewis Thompson

Available this May wherever
Harlequin and Silhouette books are sold.

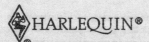 

Free Gift Offer

With a Free Gift proof-of-purchase
from any Harlequin® book, you can receive
a beautiful cubic zirconia pendant.

This stunning marquise-shaped stone is a genuine cubic
zirconia—accented by an 18" gold tone necklace.
(Approximate retail value $19.95)

Send for yours today...
compliments of ◆HARLEQUIN®

To receive your free gift, a cubic zirconia pendant, send us one original proof-of-purchase, photocopies not accepted, from the back of any Harlequin Romance®, Harlequin Presents®, Harlequin Temptation®, Harlequin Superromance®, Harlequin Intrigue®, Harlequin American Romance®, or Harlequin Historicals® title available at your favorite retail outlet, together with the Free Gift Certificate, plus a check or money order for $1.65 U.S./$2.15 CAN. (do not send cash) to cover postage and handling, payable to Harlequin Free Gift Offer. We will send you the specified gift. Allow 6 to 8 weeks for delivery. Offer good until December 31, 1997, or while quantities last. Offer valid in the U.S. and Canada only.

Free Gift Certificate

Name: _____

Address: _____

City: _____ State/Province: _____ Zip/Postal Code: _____

Mail this certificate, one proof-of-purchase and a check or money order for postage and handling to: HARLEQUIN FREE GIFT OFFER 1997. In the U.S.: 3010 Walden Avenue, P.O. Box 9071, Buffalo NY 14269-9057. In Canada: P.O. Box 604, Fort Erie, Ontario L2Z 5X3.

FREE GIFT OFFER   084-KEZ

ONE PROOF-OF-PURCHASE
To collect your fabulous FREE GIFT, a cubic zirconia pendant, you must include this
original proof-of-purchase for each gift with the properly completed Free Gift Certificate.

084-KEZR